GLANMORE;

OR,

THE BANDITS OF SARATOGA.

A Romance of the Revolution.

BY PARK CLINTON.

CINCINNATI:
PUBLISHED BY U. P. JAMES,
NO. 167 WALNUT STREET.

GLANMORE:

A ROMANCE OF THE REVOLUTION.

CHAPTER I.

Saratoga Lake—its Scenery—Snake Hill—the aged Pine—the Cave.

There are but few countries in the empire state, that can boast of more romantic associations than Saratoga, or of more beautiful scenery. True, it does not abound in those really wild and sublimely romantic scenes that characterize other portions of the state of New York, but yet there is a degree of loveliness about it, that strikes the beholder as indeed beautiful.

Among those lovely scenes, none surpass the beautiful sheet of water known as Saratoga Lake. It is situated about six miles to the south east of the far-famed Saratoga Springs. It presents a sheet of water nine miles long by four broad at its widest point. Its banks, at this time, are lined with cultivated farms, neat farm-houses, and stately old orchards, with occasionally a tract of woodland skirting its borders; no sails whiten the bosom of this most beautiful of miniature lakes. But upon a fine morning, the light row-boats of numerous fishermen may be seen dancing upon its billows, as they glide gently forward n "trailing" for the excellent bass and pickerel with which it abounds. Its appearance at this time is well known by the hundreds of the fashionable and sporting world, that resort to its banks to enjoy its piscatory sports.

To those, the high round hill on its eastern shore, covered with a luxuriant growth of timber, can be no stranger, towering as it does, far above its otherwise gently sloping shore. It is not, however, our purpose to speak minutely, or at great length, of the scenery connected with this crystal lake, at this period of time, but of events that took place while its banks were covered with the dark primeval forests, composed for the most part of towering oaks, pines, and chesnut, that cast their dark and sombre shade far over its silvery waters; of that period, when the wild deer grazed upon its banks, and the bear was wont to traverse its bosom, when winter's frosts had congealed its limpid waters, when the huge rattle-snake abounded on the before-mentioned eminence—and being found there in vast numbers, by the early settlers of old Saratoga, they gave it the truly and forbidding cognomen of Snake Hill. The fish-houses that now abound upon its shores for the accommodation of parties of ladies and gentlemen from Saratoga Springs and the neighboring cities and villages, had not then been reared; and, instead of its waters being covered at times, as they now are, by gay and joyous boat-loads of fashion and beauty, they were only occasionally called into requisition to buoy up the lone canoe of some solitary Indian.

Near the western foot of Snake Hill, grew an aged pine; ah, it was a majestic old tree!—its trunk was several feet in diameter, and it reared its lofty head far away up in the heavens; so tall and so stately did it stand, that the brain reeled, as one attempted to look up at its top from its base—and then too, it was a remarkable tree, it had withstood the whirlwinds—and its deep green foilage had been whitened with the frosts of more than two centuries, like the hero of a hundred battles, it stood in lofty, silent, and sombre grandeur—towering far above the other members of the forest—save when the winds sported with its moss-covered branches, or moaned through its evergreen foilage. The scathing lightnings had darted over its head, and the awful thunder-bolt had riven many a stalwart tree, during its time. The panther had lain upon its ponderous branches, and uttered his moaning wail, the red son of the forest had used its trunk as a secret covert from whence to send the arrow whizzing to the heart of his enemy, and yet there it stood, like the aged man, at whose vitals disease has been gnawing for years, but who is yet erect in carriage and stately in mien.

Its time, however, was drawing rapidly to a close, its trunk, although exhibiting no outward signs of decay, was, notwithstanding, hollow within, and in the year 1777, was made to subserve an unholy purpose.

Its hollow cavity was a ventilator to the dark cave of an outlaw—of a Tory Robber, who prowled with his gang of unprincipled followers, about his own native county, and waged secret war against his former neighbors and associates. His cave was situated almost immediately beneath the roots of this tree, at a point where the foot of Snake Hill reached the bold and deep shore of Saratoga Lake.

This cave was no natural excavation, it was the work of human hands — the earth had all been carefully removed and buried deep down beneath the waters of Saratoga lake; and so narrow was its entrance, and so well was it concealed by overhanging evergreens, that no one could have discovered it, unless, directed to the spot by some one acquainted with its locality. Indeed so narrow was the entrance, that but one man could walk through it at a time; no human being could have lived long within it, so stagnant was the atmosphere, had it not been for the long hollow trunk of the aged pine, that was converted into a ventilator, by cutting a number of holes in the tree above the first branches, where the incisions could not easily be seen from the ground. A small horizontal shaft had been dug from the main room in the cave, to the foot of the tree, communicating under ground, with the cavity in its trunk; a current of air was thus kept drawing constantly through the cave; and was controlled by means of a door placed at the mouth of the horizontal shaft; it was a well planned and well constructed secret subterraneous abode, from whence issued, during the summer of 1777, the year that the approaching army of Burgoyne spread terror through northern New York, almost nightly, a band of thirty Tories that spread death and consternation in their nightly track.

CHAPTER II.

Gordon Glanmore—The hypocritical old Tory—Organization of the Snake Hill Bandits.

The leader of the band that occupied this cave, was Gordon Glanmore; he was the son of a farmer, residing between Saratoga lake, and the battle ground whereon the heroes of the American Revolution met, fought, and conquered, England's boasted General, Burgoyne.

When the American struggle for freedom, freedom from the bitter and galling yoke of British bondage, commenced, or rather when the deep up-heaving of popular sentiment—of discontent—nay, of hatred itself—to British tyranny, and British oppression, manifested themselves in such a manner, and to such a degree, that a distinct line of demarcation was drawn between the advocates of freedom and independence, and the advocates of British rule and British oppression, Gordon Glanmore was found advocating the principles of the former, although at heart he was a rank Tory.

His father, a man stricken in years, although secretly favorable to English rule, yet, when called upon openly to declare his sentiments, with deep, and damning hypocrisy, gave his neighbors, who were principally Revolutionists, the strongest assurance that language could convey, that his heart was with them, in their arduous struggle for liberty; and that his hand should be found wielding the musket, or broad-sword in defence of freedom, if time had not ere this robbed him of his ability to mingle in the strife of battle, and combat the hireling minions of England. He at the same time, resolved within himself, that his son should in no event take up arms in defence of the Colonies. He labored to imbue his mind with a thorough and deep conviction, of the superiority of British rule, and British measures, over those wild schemes of Republicanism, as he termed the views of American Revolutionists. Fearing in the event of his son taking up arms in favor of England, that his father's infidelity to whig principles and sentiments might be discovered, he resolved upon an expedient that should serve him as a pretext for not entering the American army.

He was well aware at this time, that as his son professed to be a whig, he would soon be called upon to enter the American army; and resolved that the precautionary measures necessary to prevent such a result, should be immediately taken. He had so thoroughly warped the mind of his son, that from at first having slightly favored the Colonists, he finally became so strongly opposed to them that he was urgent in his solicitations to be permitted to join the Royal army.

His father represented to him, the utter ruin that would fall upon him, should the Americans finally triumph; and in furtherance of his plan for preventing his joining the Royal army, intimated that if he wished to make actual war upon the whigs, he might do so in a secret way, and in a manner that would redound to his profit; he could easily raise a band of Tories, a small, select number, from the adjoining country; they could find some place among the deep and dark pine forests of Saratoga, where they could dig a cave, and as the population was exceedingly sparse, they might be effectually hidden there from observation. They could make nightly excursions, fall upon those Whig families who were reputed to have money hoarded in their houses, and as they would fall easy victims to them, they might before the close of the war, amass a splendid fortune for the whole band.

Gordon Glanmore being naturally of an avaricious disposition, soon fell in with his father's suggestions. The party lines had now become so strongly drawn between the Whigs and Tories, that the fiercest hatred rankled in their breasts against each other. Glanmore could no longer remain inactive. The tide of war rolled on, and as hundreds of brave patriots were falling from the ranks of the American army, by "war, pestilence and famine," others were called upon to supply their places and he could openly carry out his double dealing no longer.

His father was in secret communication with a number of Tories, who were pursuing the same secret course with regard to the war, as himself. Secretly they were summoned to meet at his house,—in a short time a meeting took place—at midnight—upon the first dark and stormy night after the notice given—did these hypocritical Tories assemble at the house of Gordon Glanmore's father. The windows were muffled, and with low voices, they coolly deliberated upon the best method of organizing a band of stealthy robbers, with Gordon Glanmore as a leader, to murder and rob their unsuspecting neighbors.

The band was organized; it consisted of ten men, Glanmore was chosen chief of the band by a unanimous vote, he was to receive one third of all the booty, and they in turn, swore fidelity to him, and to each other, until death should separate them.

They next deliberated upon the best method of putting their plans in execution. Glanmore's father being the originator of the plan for raising the band, was listened to with profound attention. The young men who composed the band, coming from various parts of the country, suggested various points that, in their judgment, would be favorable locations for a rendezvous, from whence they could carry on their depredations most successfully.

The elder Glanmore having been a surveyor, and having also hunted over most of the adjoining country, suggested that there was no place that he knew of so well adapted to the purpose as Snake Hill, an eminence on the shore of Saratoga Lake. It was covered with a dense forest. It was a lonely and retired spot; and besides it was so infested with Rattlesnakes, that people always avoided it, unless when necessity compelled them to visit it.

The shore of the lake was there bold and deep. A cave could be dug into the hill-side, with a narrow entrance. The earth taken from it could be sunk in the deep water of the lake, and if he was not mistaken, the evergreens growing thickly along the bank, would effectually screen the entrance of the cave from observation, both in winter and summer. His advice was adopted. The company separated, and by daylight were far on their journeys towards their respective residences. Morning dawned, and Gordon Glanmore, with a cousin of his, who had tarried under the pretext of visiting his uncle's family, fully equipped, sallied forth, ostensibly for the purpose of hunting, but really for the purpose of repairing io Saratoga Lake, and examining Snake Hill as a future hiding place for the band, who were to carry out the dark resolves they had formed the preceding night.

They found it all that could be desired. It was as it had been represented, an excellent location for them—and to be breif, with the assistance of part of the gang, who were soon summoned, they, by working during the nights of the next fortnight, finished the excavation of the cave.

CHAPTER III.

Plan of the old Tory for accounting for his son's absence —Purchase of a horse—pretends to send him to Westchester — Glanmore reaches the cave by a circuitous route, and becomes the bandit of Snake Hill.

All the arrangements at the cave being completed, the next, and most difficult point to be decided was, as to how they were to up keep the deception towards the Whigs. If they should retire to the cave, would not those Whigs who considered them their friends, inquire where they were gone? If their families represented to their Whig neighbors, that they were gone to the American Army, would not some one of the numerous soldiers, who were constantly coming home from the army, wounded and otherwise, soon acquaint them with the fact that they were in no part of the American army? True, this might not occur, but still it was positively necessary that some excuse should be held forth, for the disappearance of Glanmore.

He would gladly have remained at his home, and rendezvoused at the cave as occasion required, but a crisis had now arrived, when he must either declare himself a Tory openly, join the American army, or take up his residence permanently at the secret cave at Snake Hill. The latter course being of course resolved on, the following deep laid plot was hit upon in order to satisfy the curiosity of Glanmore's Whig neighbors, as well as to lull all suspicions that might possibly be entertained with reference to him; for in those troublesome times every man kept a strict watch upon all suspicious movements of his neighbors, that could not be strictly accounted for. Old Glanmore gave out that he had some business of importance, that must be attended to, near the City of New York; and much as he deplored the stern necessity of the case, yet he was obliged to send his son to attend to it; and as in those days there were no steamboats or railroads, the most expeditious mode of performing the journey would be on horseback. In order effectually to blind the eyes of the Whigs, he went to one of his neighbors, and purchased of him a large and powerful horse, celebrated for his speed, that was to serve his son to escape from any English scouts that might possibly fall in with him, as his business would lead very near the British lines, above New York.

The day was fixed upon for his departure—he did depart, but not for Westchester, as had been held out. Mounted on this powerful steed, he rode away, with friendly greetings of farewell from his neighbors—those neighbors who he then designed to rob and murder, the first opportunity that should offer.

The old Tory looked after his son, and as one of his Whig neighbors stood by, brushed a hypocritical tear from his eye, as he adverted to the possibility of his son being captured by the British, or killed by the hand of some ruthless Tory.

Three weeks passed away, and no tidings of Gordon Glanmore were received. At length one fine and cloudless morning, the self same steed that he rode away, was seen approaching the house of one of Glanmore's Whig neighbors, and halting, his rider inquired for old Glanmore's residence.

Great was the excitement when it was rumored that a man from Westchester had arrived with Gordon Glanmore's horse, that Glanmore had been surprised by a body of British cavalry, that being wounded, he fell from his horse, and was captured, that the horse escaped, and that Glanmore declaring himself boldly to be a Whig, had been carried to New York, and was now a prisoner within the British lines.

The man who brought back the horse, also exhibited a letter, purporting to come from Glanmore's uncle, who resided in Westchester. The letter read as follows:

WESTCHESTER, June, 1777.

Dear Brother,—Your son Gordon arrived here two weeks since; we were much pleased to hear from you and your family. I regret that I am under the necessity of informing you that he is a prisoner within the British lines. After tarrying with us a few days, he set out to visit the person with whom he was to transact the business you entrusted to him. We were greatly surprised to see the fine horse he rode, come galloping back a few hours afterwards, with his saddle and bridle on; we caught the horse, and discovered blood upon the saddle; we supposed that poor Gordon had been killed by some of the Tories, who are lurking about, and watching every opportunity to destroy the Whigs. We raised a company and started out, supposing that we might possibly find him killed or wounded; not succeeding, however, in finding him, we gave him up for lost.

We were relieved, however, from our apprehensions concerning him, by the receipt a few days after, of the enclosed letter, that he found means of sending to us. By perusing it you will get the truth with regard to his disappearance. I return the horse by the bearer, a young Whig neighbor of mine.

Your Brother,
JAMES GLANMORE.

JOHN GLANMORE.

The enclosed letter, purporting to come from Gordon Glanmore, after his capture, to his uncle, in Westchester, read as follows:

NEW YORK, June, 1777.

Dear Uncle,—I am now a prisoner in New York. After leaving your house, I travelled on a few miles towards the place of my destination; suddenly, as I emerged from a thick dark wood, I came full upon a company of fourteen British horsemen. They ordered me to halt, and immediately commenced a search of my person; they accused me of being a spy, as soon as I told them I was from Saratoga; finding they were likely to take me to New York, I attempted to escape, trusting that the superior speed of my horse would enable me to do so, but a ball from one of their pistols stunned me, and I fell from my horse. I was carried to the city, and taken before one of their officers; disdaining to conceal my principles, I owned myself to be a Whig; I am here in close custody.

You will please acquaint my father, with my situation, as soon as possible.

Your Nephew,
GORDON GLANMORE.

JAMES GLANMORE.

The neighbors soon flocked to the house of old Glanmore, to console him in the hour of his affliction, and deeply did they deplore the loss of so brave a young man, who would have been so valuable a soldier in the Continental army. They commended his spirit in not flinching or recanting when brought before the British officer; and attempted to console him with the idea that his son, not being taken in arms, would speedily be released, and return home, when he would have an opportunity of joining the American army, and wreaking his vengeance on the dastardly English. The old man appeared inconsolable for the loss of his son, but as soon as his neighbors were out of sight, he turned to the man who had brought back the horse, and with a knowing wink beckoned him to follow to an adjoining room.

As soon as they were seated, he exclaimed, "Don't you

think we have hit upon a capital plan for covering Gordon's absence?"

"First rate," returned the man, rubbing his hands with evident delight. "How they swallowed the contents of them letters; and how they will be sympathizing with poor Gordon, in his imaginary imprisonment."

"Well," said old Glanmore, "I suppose by this time, you have got all things arranged at the cave?"

"All in order for business," said the man.

"How did Gordon make out in getting there?" said the old man.

"Oh, capital;" returned the man, "after he left home he kept on for some distance towards Albany; when he reached the pine lands on the north of the Mohawk, he plunged into the woods, and after riding two nights, reached the residence of one of the band. There the horse was kept in a close stable until we thought that time enough had elapsed, to make your plans seem probable. I was then sent from the cave to bring the horse back, and the forged letters and false news."

This plan effectually screened Glanmore from suspicion among his Whig neighbors.

CHAPTER IV.

Glanmore's secret passion — The fires of love, jealousy and revenge, smoulder in his bosom — Caroline Mansfield — her personal charms — Glanmore's endeavors to win her — His rival, George Rushwood, the widow's son.

Our hero being now snugly quartered in his secret cave, at Snake Hill, and having become invested with the command of a company of stalwart brigands, it would indeed be out of the general order of things, if he had left behind him no image of maiden fair; that now haunted him in his solitary cave. And we trow that many a maiden's heart has been caused to beat more quickly, at beholding a bandit chief, less comely and commanding than he.

We have already said, that avaricious propensities, aided by the influence of his father, had led him to assume his present position; but yet it will be seen hereafter, that other sentiments and passions than those of avarice, exerted a strong and overwhelming influence over him; and indeed so much was he influenced by them, and to such an extent did they lead him, that those acts perpetrated by him, while under their influence, form by far the most startling, interesting, and romantic part of his subsequent history. These passions were love, jealousy, and revenge. They were aroused in his bosom in early life, and as the object that created them seemed to recede farther and farther from his grasp, they increased in strength, until, at the period when he took up his quarters at Snake Hill, they burned with an ardor that nothing short of death itself, seemed capable of extinguishing. In the same neighborhood with our hero, lived a young and beautiful maiden; she was the only daughter of one of the wealthiest and most influential Whigs in that section of the country. He was a descendant of the puritans of New England, of those men who first raised the standard of the cross on Plymouth rock. In early life he married an English lady of wealth, who, bringing with her from her native country many of those higher and more refined accomplishments, that were but little known or practiced by the wives of backwoodsmen at that time, she instilled them into her daughter's mind with such studious care, that when

Caroline Mansfield reached her eighteenth year, she was justly acknowledged to be the most enlightened and highly accomplished young lady within the sphere of her acquaintance.

As we have before intimated, Gordon Glanmore was deeply in love with this interesting girl, and had he possessed principles of the right stamp, we could find no fault with him for indulging such sentiments towards her; for in addition to those accomplishments we have before mentioned, so extremely rare at that period, especially among the daughters of the yeomanry, she possessed charms that might have captivated hearts still less susceptible than that of Gordon Glanmore. True, she did not possess that exquisitely and delicately refined feminine beauty, that is made the standard of female beauty by many; yet, perhaps, this might have been accounted for, by the peculiar circumstances under which she was reared. For, although educated in many of the higher and more refined departments of Literature and Art, yet she had been permitted to roam freely, with the neighboring farmers' daughters, over the green fields of old Saratoga, to pull the wild flowers, and ramble through the deep and dark pine forests in search of such amusements as are always pleasing and invigorating, to the true lover of nature, in her pristine purity. These rural exercises had given her naturally fine form, an exquisite development, and imparted to her cheek a ruddy glow, that many a highly accomplished, yet faded and enervated modern young lady might justly be proud of. Her hair fell in wild, luxuriant ringlets about her shoulders; and when she bounded with fawn-like activity, with her young companions, her wild musical laugh seemed to impart to their minds, the same degree of buoyant happiness that gushed forth from her own. And if, when she thus laughed, she showed her English origin, by displaying a mouth too wide, to be considered truly elegant, yet this defect was more than remedied, by the exposure at the same time, of a set of teeth, rivalling in point of whiteness and exquisite polish, the purest ivory.

But if in point of personal beauty and accomplisments, Caroline Mansfield outrivalled her young companions, she certainly, in point of deep discriminating judgment, entirely transcended and totally eclipsed them.

Glanmore had conceived his passion for her in his boyhood; and although his attentions were unceasing, yet, he totally failed to make that favorable impression upon her; and to win from her in return for his attentions, that encouraging smile and manner that he so much coveted. Knowing her love for the wild flowers of the forest, he plucked the first blown, and hastened to present them to her. Did he in his rambles through the forest, discover a bush uncommonly laden with fruit, it was cut from its root with the greatest care, so that not a single berry might be lost, and conveyed to her. Did he succeed in capturing a young bird, it was soon caged, and taught to sing its sweetest notes for his loved, though not loving Caroline. Arduously as did our young hero pursue his object, he not only found himself baffled, but actually had a formidable rival in the person of George Rushwood, a youth who was the son of a poor widow, residing in the immediate neighborhood of Glanmore and Miss Mansfield. His father was likewise a descendant of the old New England stock, and fell bravely fighting under the heroic and much lamented Wolf, on the plains of Abraham. Rushwood was then but an infant; and to him did his widowed mother cling with all that parental anxiety, that none but a widowed mother can possibly feel. She struggled against the bitter trials and pinching wants of poverty; and with heroic fortitude, succeeded, in conveying him across the Rubicon of helplessness.

She labored to imbue his mind with correct and noble principles; and with the scanty means at her command, succeeded in giving him the first rudiments of an education. When he reached his twelfth year, he saw with what difficulty his widowed mother managed to sustain him; and with the high-souled purpose of relieving her from the burden, and contributing to her future support and happiness, he resolved at once to seek some business, that might furnish him with the means of so doing. To this end he sought employment from Caroline Mansfield's father, and readily obtained it. This gentleman was well satisfied with his industry, and disposition to please. He observed, moreover, that when at the end of a harvesting, or other laborious job, he gave his "hands" a "play day," George, instead of mingling with them in hunting and fishing, their usual avocations at such seasons, always repaired to his mother's residence and spent the day working in her garden, or in making such repairs about her cottage, as would render it more comfortable and pleasant; and when upon a rainy day, or during a long evening, his other hands would amuse themselves by dancing or playing cards in an old barn, or in murdering some tune on an old crazy fiddle, George would be seen to steal off into some quiet corner, and pore over the pages of some old book, that had been handed down from his grandfather's library.

Mr. Mansfield, perceiving the literary taste manifested by young Rushwood, kindly offered him the privilege of his library, a privilege which was highly prized by him, and of which he took the utmost possible advantage.

In a few years Rushwood by his industry amassed a sufficient amount of money to purchase a fifty acre lot, and set up farming on his own account, in which he was kindly aided by Mr. Mansfield.

But his becoming master of the soil upon which he labored, did not quench his insatiable desire for knowledge. He delighted to roam through the pages of ancient history; and, aided by Mrs. Mansfield, mastered the French language to such an extent as to be able to speak it quite fluently.

Nearly every week did Rushwood repair to the residence of Mr. Mansfield, to either borrow or return some volume; and is it strange to relate, that he too actually became deeply smitten with the charms of the lovely and beautiful Caroline Mansfield?

Glanmore was not insensible of the power of his rival, for although poor in purse, he was, notwithstanding, rich in intellectual wealth, when compared with him.

He sought to arrest the current of Miss Mansfield's feelings, that he too plainly saw was setting strongly towards George Rushwood; and to effect this, lost no opportunity of lessening him in Miss Mansfield's estimation.

She, however, wisely kept her own counsel, knowing full well, that although her father admired the industrious and sterling qualities of Rushwood, yet his proud, haughty spirit, would never brook the idea of his daughter even looking with favor upon one who had been a hireling in his house, and who owed much of his success to his bounty.

And should she endeavor to set up her own will in the matter, in opposition to that of her father, his strict puritanical notions of a daughter's duty towards a parent, would overwhelm her with a force perfectly irresistible. She was too young to think of receiving the particular addresses of any one, but yet young as she was, she believed her heart to be irrevocably placed upon George Rushwood; and acting under the influence of this belief, she received his attentions with a secret pleasure, that however much she endeavored to conceal, would occasionally reveal itself, in the tell-tale countenance.

CHAPTER V.

Glanmore's jealousy aroused—sends Miss Mansfield a bouquet —comes near going mad with excitement—makes a fearful resolve against George Rushwood—determines to bide his time.

THUS stood matters, when these two young men reached their twentieth year.

It was a bright and beautiful evening, in the month of April, when a joyous party were assembled at the house of a farmer in their immediate neighborhood. All the comely young lassies in the neighborhood, and indeed for some distance around, were there.

This was not one of those fashionable gatherings, known as parties in these days of refinement, but one of those gatherings of young people, known in that day as "Spinning Bees." As our modern young ladies may never have had the pleasure of attending one of those convivial assemblies, we will in this place, for their especial gratification, endeavor to give them a description of this one, in which one of our heros was particularly interested. As an introduction, however, we will state, that the young ladies of that period, when the clangor of arms and the thunder of British and American artillery reverberated along the valleys, and among the hills of our bleeding country, were well versed in the use of certain domestic implements, known in common parlance as the "great and little wheel," which said implements were to be found in nearly every domicile of our ancestors; but have, of late years, given place to the more refined and musical piece of furniture, to wit: the Piano. We said the more musical piece of furniture, but yet perhaps the low-moaning hum of the country maiden's spinning wheel was quite as pleasing to the ear, (since it was connected with visions of "nice warm woolen stockings," "drugget gowns," and huge "bear skin coats," and long pieces of linen, to be whitened upon the velvet lawn, when the sun's rays should be sufficiently intense for that purpose,) as the murderous performances upon the piano, that now greet the ear of the pedestrian while perambulating the streets of our large cities, and remote country villages; or bore his patience while calling upon, or visiting those families, where anxious mammas are crowding their daughters around the piano, for the purpose of having their horrible performances eulogized, and of displaying their wonderful dexterity in fingering the keys; and drawing forth the dulcet sounds of music rare, that they design one day or other to bring to bear upon the heart of some susceptible swain..

Be this, however, as it may, an old lady who had several daughters, had come to the conclusion to have a "Spinning Bee," and the party mentioned had been drawn together in the usual manner, which was as follows: A large quantity of Flax was given out in quantities of several pounds each, to certain young men about the neighborhood. They in turn, distributed this flax, in small quantities, to such young ladies about the country, as would be likely to attend the "Bee," with an invitation to attend, at a certain time then specified.

Now if the young ladies accepted the Flax, they of course accepted the invitation; and it then became their imperative duty to spin the flax into yarn, and have the yarn and themselves ready, on the day mentioned, to be borne on the cruppers of their beaux' saddles, to the place where the "Bee" was to be held; for in those days when the roads were full of stumps, travelling on horseback was the most usual and indeed fashionable mode of progress.

We would not have our fashionable young friends believe that our ancestors indulged in any such vulgar occupations as "spinning yarn," after they had thus "then and there assembled;" true, some old spinsters that were generally "on hand," for the purpose of receiving the various parcels of "yarn," would indulge in "spinning" rather "long yarns" on the workmanship of the various young ladies, but as those were nearly analogous to "street yarns," we are of opinion that a recital of them would not interest a modern reader.

No, the young people of that day did not indulge in spinning at parties of pleasure. And a "Spinning Bee" was strictly such; but they killed time very much as the moderns do, principally by endeavoring to ascertain which of the company could perpetrate the greatest amount of folly in a given time, and as for spinning or any other kind of labor;

"O no, they never mentioned it"

Neither did they masticate "sour grapes" or "musty almonds," or get "boozy" on "port wine" or "champagne" that had never seen salt water. But they made ample amends for the want of these refined delicacies, by drinking the pure juice of the "red streak," and masticating "golden apples," that had been husbanded with great care "a purpose for the Spinning Bee," and one very rational amusement of the young ladies consisted in paring off the rind of the apple, and after swinging it a number of times around their heads, throwing it down, and imagining what letter of the alphabet it most resembled; which said letter the fates decreed, should be the first letter of the name of him, who was to be the husband of the thrower. As for the supper, it did not consist, as a popular writer has asserted the suppers of the old New Netherlanders did, of a dish of fat pork, and a lump of sugar suspended by a string, and left swinging over the table;—but of roasted fowls and turkeys, huge mince pies, and mountain piles of "sap cakes," smoking hot, and sap coffee to match; and delicate little china cups of continental tea, that was made of a shrub common in the northern colonies, and furnished the patriotic ladies who voluntarily banished tea from their tables, quite a fragrant substitute therefor.

A goodly number, as we before said, were congregated at this "Spinning Bee," but yet there was evidently a blank. The reigning spirit, she who was the cynosure of all eyes upon such occasions, was absent; and although it was a season of gayety and mirthfulness, yet the inquiry was frequently repeated, "why is Miss Mansfield not here?" and then the oft repeated tale that Caroline Mansfield was indisposed, and had been for some time, was eagerly told by some one who wished to make herself conspicuous by repeating the name of her who would have monopolized in spite of herself, the greater share of attention had she been present.

And then the remark was made, that, perhaps, Miss Mansfield's not being able to attend the "Bee," was the cause of George Rushwood's not being there; and then certain sly hints were thrown out in relation to the mutual attachment between these two young people.

Gordon Glanmore overheard these remarks, together with certain additions and variations, that reflected upon his own unsuccessful attachment to the same young lady. They stung him to the quick; his enjoyment, for the balance of the evening, was blasted and withered, under the influence of the reflection that his hated and despised rival, the poor old widow Rushbrook's son, had so far supplanted him, that it had become the subject of jocular remark among his young associates. He endeavored to throw off his sad reflections, but his efforts were of no avail; he returned home in no very amiable, or, indeed, enviable mood.

The next morning was one of those mild April mornings,

when the swelling buds, and wild flowers, peering from among the withered and strewn foliage of the preceding year, warn us that nature is about to appear again, robed in garments of green, and bedecked with brilliant flowers. The mild zephyr gently fanned the cheek, and sported with the glossy locks of Gordon Glanmore, as he wended his way across the broad fields of his father's domain, towards an enclosure, wherein was confined a flock of snow-white lambs, that were gayly sporting around their dams. He fed his father's flock, and as he was returning towards home, he passed through a small piece of woodland, where, upon a bank, above a murmuring brook, he perceived upon the sunny side, a few scattering wild flowers. The gentle murmur of the sparkling waters, that seemed leaping along over the pebbly bottom for very joy, the distant roar of the Mohawk, that was now swollen and rapid, and came wafted on the wings of the mild south-westerly breeze, all contributed to soothe his troubled spirit into calmness. He plucked the wild flowers; and, as he arranged them into a bouquet, a thought struck him. He recollected that his sister had expressed an intention of calling on Miss Mansfield that very morning; he would send the bunch of wild flowers to her by the hands of his sister, with his compliments.

When he returned to the house, his sister already had on her bonnet and shawl; handing her the bouquet, he requested her to present it to Miss Mansfield, as the first floral offering of the season.

When his sister returned home, he enquired after Miss Mansfield's health, and, at the same time, whether she seemed pleased with his floral offering. But, alas! the tidings she brought only added another, and more bitter pang, to his heart.

George Rushwood had been there but a few moments before she arrived. He had also brought an offering of the first wild flowers of the season. They were carefully placed in a small vase.

Start not, gentle reader, nor think that this matter of giving and receiving simple wild flowers, was a childish, or an insipid thing. Did you ever read the beautiful lines of Tuckerman:

> "One wild flower, from the path of love,
> All lowly though it lie,
> Is dearer than the wreath that waves,
> To stern ambition's eye."

When she presented Glanmore's bouquet, Miss Mansfield received them with a faint smile, and placed them upon a small work-table by which she was sitting, without bestowing upon them the care she had upon those received from Rushwood.

Glanmore left the house with a palpitating heart; the blood forsook his cheek. He wandered on he knew not where; across the fields, through the forest glade went he;—endeavoring to come to some definite conclusion in regard to this affair of love. Deep and bitter were the denunciations he gave vent to, in muttering tones, with clenched fists and grating teeth. The worst passions of the human heart were aroused in him. Sometimes he resolved to do one thing, and sometimes another. To challenge George Rushwood to mortal combat, or by some grand stratagem to undermine his character, and bring his name so far beneath the overwhelming waves of public scorn, that he could never rise from their blasting influence.

Before he actually knew where he was going, or how far he had wandered, he found himself beyond the residence of Mr. Mansfield. With feelings of extreme mortification, he turned back into the highway, and wended his way homeward. As he passed the house of Mr. Mansfield, he could not refrain from looking towards the window, to catch, if possible, a nod of recognition from the object of his solicitude. But, instead of getting even a glimpse of Miss Mansfield, he beheld the bouquet he had arranged with so much care, lying near the door, where it had been thrown by some sacrilegious hand. "Can it be possible," he mentally exclaimed, "that Miss Mansfield has shown such a striking and absolute preference for Rushwood?" He would know immediately; and, upon some slight pretence, he entered the house, where almost the first object that met his view, was the flowers presented by his rival. He was almost paralyzed; the blood mounted to his temples, and he was on the point of giving vent to a torrent of invective against the character of his rival.

But, suddenly checking himself, he made some enquiries of Mr. Mansfield about certain farm stock, that he alleged had strayed from his father's premises, and left the house, vowing to be revenged upon his successful rival. As he went along, he recollected that a sanguinary war was then existing between Great Britain and his native country. The day would soon come when his rival, as he was a Whig, would be obliged to enter the army. Possibly he might be slain there; but if he was not, he, yes, he, might, under the circumstances, kill him with impunity; as, according to the theory of Toryism, there was no moral turpitude attached to the act of killing a Whig. He would wreak his vengeance upon him before the close of the war, and then the way to Caroline Mansfield's heart would be open to him.

With this resolve he determined to bide his time; and when his father urged upon him the propriety of not joining the

British army, after George Rushwood had expressed a determination to enlist under the American banner, he listened with a great degree of satisfaction to his plans, as by being in that position, he could keep spies upon Caroline, and, if matters were likely to come to a final issue between her and Rushwood, he could, he trusted, find means of putting an end to him, and thus prevent their union. This being the state of his mind, at the time he entered his subterranean quarters at Snake Hill, it is easy to conceive that other passions than that of avarice, had a strong and controlling influence over him.

CHAPTER VI.

George Rushwood's Whig Principles — Glanmore conceals his deadly Enmity to Rushwood — Makes frequent Visits at Mansfield's — Philosophizes on the probably favorable termination of his Love matters—Rushwood resolves to join the American Army — His Mother opposes him at first, but, finally encourages him — Takes a Solemn Leave of her — Calls on Miss Mansfield — Their Secret Betrothal—Takes leave of her, and goes to the American Army.

THE future fortunes of Glanmore and Rushwood having now become blended, it will be necessary to take a retrospective view of the conduct of Rushwood, with reference to the fierce struggle for independence.

When, in the spring of 1775, the news of the battle of Lexington spread through the country, every heart was aroused; and, among the youth whose hearts beat in unison with the struggling Colonists, none took a more manly, open, and decided stand than George Rushwood.

His extensive reading had made him acquainted with the principles of democratic liberty; and with studious care he kept himself constantly informed of all the leading movements of those patriots, who were thundering their anathemas in the legislative halls of the different colonies, against British usurpations.

Mr. Mansfield also held opinions of the same character, and during the exciting period that preceded the campaign of Burgoyne, no one was more welcome at his house than Rushwood.

His daughter was found, also, warmly advocating the principles of freedom.

Glanmore was, during this time, a frequent visitor at the

house of Mr. Mansfield; and, when the conversation turned upon public affairs, he did not scruple to openly declare himself as deeply sympathizing with the Whigs; although, at heart, as base a Tory as ever polluted the free air of America.

He was, at times, nearly beside himself with the fierce passions of love, jealousy, and revenge, all pent up and smouldering in his bosom at once, yet since he came to his last fearful resolve of taking the life of Rushwood before the close of the war, he managed to control himself with such extreme caution and apparent coolness, that no one suspected him of maintaining toward his rival, any very decided bitter feelings; he was aided in this by the reflection that although Miss Mansfield manifested a decided preference for Rushwood, yet he knew the feelings with which her father looked down upon him, and he firmly believed that he would not consent to his daughter's marrying one so much beneath her in point of pecuniary wealth. He trusted, therefore, that he could accomplish the ruin of Rushwood before the close of the war, and until that time he feared no decided steps, on the part of Miss Mansfield, with regard to matrimony, as at that period so undecided were people with reference to the final issue of the war, especially on the northern borders near Canada, that they thought more about the prospect of being butchered, especially the Whigs, by the hands of the prowling Tories, the British soldiery, and the fierce savages attached to the British interest, than they did of "marrying, or giving in marriage."

He laid it down therefore as a self-evident truth, that Miss Mansfield would be unmarried at the close of the war, and if he could succeed in destroying his rival, and concealing his opposition to whig principles from her father, he should then have the field entirely to himself, and besides, he would have the influence of her father in his behalf, as he had in sundry ways manifested a tacit willingness that his daughter should receive his addresses.

Rushwood adhered to his whig principles with the utmost ardor, and in the Spring of 1777, the same year that Glanmore became the bandit of Snake Hill, resolved to join the American army, and assist his struggling countrymen in arresting the course of Burgoyne and the British allies. He made his intentions known to his mother, who, although a strong advocate for freedom, wavered at first when she recollected that her husband, but a few brief years before, had fallen in the French war. The mangled and bleeding corpse of her darling son rose up in imagination before her, and although at the same time she could reasonably suppose that he might return to her unharmed, and crowned with laurels won in defence of the rights of his native land, yet the feelings of the mother for a time prevailed over those of the patriotic woman.

But when the news came that Burgoyne was actually advancing—when the inquiry among the inhabitants of the country that lay in the track he designed to pursue—began to be, whether they should rush spontaneously to arms, and repel their boasting invaders; or whether they should fly with their families into New England;—Mrs Rushwood hesitated no longer: "go," said she to her son, "go, George, and fight manfully the battles of your country—go, for although you may face death in a thousand forms, yet I feel assured that the cause in which you will be engaged is a righteous one; I am also assured that God is the God of battles, as well as the God of peace, and that your life is in his hands, whether amid the thunder and crash of battle, or peaceably turning the furrows upon your farm—yes, go, my son, and imitate the proud example of your departed sire, who fell in the front rank, bravely leading on his followers to victory." And George Rushwood did go—yes, he went forth to face the proud and vaunting hosts of Britain.

Never did the sun shine upon a more glorious morning than that of the first day of June, 1777, when he took his departure from his humble yet happy home. He determined to join the cavalry, as there seemed to be something more consonant with his nature in the idea of charging the enemy, mounted upon a noble steed.

Early on that morning he wended his way across his little farm towards a field in which his only horse, a strong and active bay, was cropping the green herbage at his leisure. As he went along, he surveyed his well-fenced inclosures, and gazed at many a huge stump from which the mighty forest tree had been hewn by his own stalwart arms; these inanimate objects, with which he had grown familiar, seemed now like so many old and familiar friends, from whom he was to part perhaps forever; and it seemed to him, as though the thrush that had been accustomed to repeat his whistle, as he trudged merrily along behind his plough, sung in a more plaintive strain than usual, and when he reached the bars, that led out of the lot wherein his petted steed was grazing, and when the gallant bay came bounding up to him expecting his usual dainty bit of salt or corn, he heaved an involuntary sigh, as he thought of the terrible fate that perhaps awaited both horse and master: and as he led the noble and docile beast forth from his peaceful pasture, he mentally exclaimed, "Ah, poor Pompey! I fear that you will never again be permitted to graze these little fields of mine; but still, if you behave yourself right gallantly, and bear me through the carnage of battle unharmed till smiling peace again dawns upon our country, you shall be a pensioner, and roam at will over the green fields of my little farm."

When his sleek and restive horse was fastened at his mother's door, he entered her humble abode, and slowly commenced packing his valise—not a word was spoken either by him or his mother—with mechanical precision she moved about, and placed before him such articles as she had prepared for him,—and when he had enveloped his tall manly form in the uniform of a trooper, she opened a chest and took therefrom a heavy steel-scabbard sword—the sword of her husband, that had been brought back to her by the hands of a fellow-soldier of his—all red with the blood of the foeman.—She approached her son—she buckled it upon him with her own hands—but yet she spoke not—no, that mother's heart was too full for utterance—she was about to offer her only child, her darling child a sacrifice upon the altar of her country, and although she acted upon the faith of a high and stern sense of duty, yet her heart was well-nigh bursting—the fountain of her tears seemed frozen, dried up, and when she kneeled to offer up a prayer to the most high God, in behalf of her son who was now about to go forth to the battle-field—Ah, and when he too kneeled by her side—her heart was yet too full for utterance, silently she addressed the throne of grace, and when that silent yet eloquent prayer was ended, she embraced the manly, athletic form of her beloved son, she received the warm farewell pressure of his lips; and when he mounted his noble steed, that curveted gayly away, as if proud of his burden and mission, she watched him with sealed lips, until his horse turned an angle in the road, skirting a piece of woodland, and was lost to view.

She stood transfixed for a few moments, and then slowly entered her dwelling. The heart that was well-nigh broken now found relief—tears flowed down those careworn and furrowed cheeks, and when she had wept herself into calmness, she knelt, and long and fervently did she pray: that if it should please her heavenly parent, he would vouchsafe to return to her arms, her only—her beloved son.

Let those who talk of disunion as a mere business affair, as a mere question of dollars and cents, pause in their reckless career, and looking back through the vista of years behold the mighty struggles; the deep heart-struggles; the self-denials; the sufferings; the hardships; the sacrifices of the best and bravest blood of the country;—in order to build up the union of these United States; and then let them check themselves, ere, with a high-wrought sectional and fanatical enthusiasm, they seek to sunder those sacred ties between the states that were cemented with the blood of thousands of patriots, and sealed with the tears of thousands of suffering widows and orphans.

When Rushwood came opposite Mr. Mansfield's house, he could not resist the desire of once more beholding Caroline, of hearing her say farewell, and of receiving from her one more of those sweet and encouraging smiles, that should nerve his arm in the hour of danger.

He halted at the door, and dismounted. Entering the house, he found Caroline alone; her father and mother having gone to attend the funeral of a friend.

"Why, really, George," said Miss Mansfield, "you present quite a soldier-like appearance; one would suppose that you were actually going to the army."

"I supposed," said George, "that it was notorious in the neighborhood that I was about to join the army; and if you are not aware of it, I now tell you, in all sincerity, that I am now actually on my way to the American camp."

Caroline turned pale; vainly she strove to hide her emotion, it was evident, that the news fell like a thunderbolt upon her. She had, it is true, heard George frequently say that he should join the army; but, then, she did not suppose that he would volunteer, especially as his mother would be left unprotected. She more than half suspected, upon consideration, that he was jesting with her, and finally recovering her composure, she said, "So you are really on your way to the army?"

"I am, positively," said George; "and I could not resist the temptation of calling on your family as I went along. I wished to say farewell to your father, and to assure him, that if I should never return, I should carry down to the grave a warm sense of gratitude, for the many deeds of kindness and benevolence, that he has manifested both towards me and my widowed mother."

"And did you not wish to say farewell to mother and me?" said Caroline. "I certainly shall be jealous, George," at the same time looking him archly in the face.

"Never fear for me, Caroline," said George, gayly; "I shall carry your image with me on the field of battle, and if a sense of your distinguished favor does not lead me to deeds of noble daring, then banish me forever from your memory."

"You speak right gallantly, sir knight," said Caroline, imitating George's manner; "and if my image is indeed so deeply graven on your heart, that it will arise before you amid the roar of battle, then take this real image of myself, (at the same time handing him a miniature painting of herself, set in a gold locket,) and wear it as a token of past and future friendship, between yourself and me."

George took the miniature with a trembling hand. Wild and tumultuous were the feelings that pervaded his bosom.—Did Caroline Mansfield really and sincerely love him, or was it merely the romantic idea of having her miniature borne through the field of battle by a soldier, that had prompted her to proffer him that beautiful talisman?

He would decide the matter now. Yes, before he mingled in the strife of battle, he would know whether his long and arduous attachment to this lovely and beautiful girl, was reciprocated on her part, or not.

"Caroline," said he, assuming a more serious air, "nothing on earth could afford me greater pleasure, than to be permitted to wear so beautiful an image of yourself; but, then"—and he paused—"could I be permitted to wear it in another and nearer character than that of a mere friend."—

Caroline blushed deeply, and was evidently much agitated. In a moment, George was by her side; and what he said—is not, dear reader, for us to write, or you to read; but this much we can assure you, that before another hour had passed upon the rapid wing of time, that always, as I presume you know by experience, flies more rapidly with lovers at such moments, than it does with people under other circumstances, they were betrothed. But why so speedily betrothed? After George had been accepted by Miss Mansfield, she informed him that her father, having perceived that she was inclined to favor him, in preference to Gordon Glanmore, who constantly persecuted her with his attentions, had forbid her receiving his attentions, or holding any intercourse with him. That previous to Glanmore's going to Westchester, he had actually solicited her hand from her father; and that she believed the match between herself and Glanmore had been finally settled between his parents and hers; and that when he returned home, they would endeavor to urge her into a marriage with him, to which she had resolved never to submit.

"I commend your course," said George; "and should do so, if I was not a party interested, for I more than half believe that he is a traitor to his country, and that instead of now being a prisoner in New York, he is either attached to some prowling band of Tories, or else in the British army."

"I am resolved, at all hazards," said Caroline, "not to marry him, as I believe him to be totally void of correct principles."

"But, suppose," said George, "that your parents insist upon

your marrying him immediately, if he should return home soon?"

"Then I will tell them, at once," said the heroic girl, "that my heart and hand are betrothed to you."

No particular time was agreed upon between the lovers, for the consummation of their vows, as that was a point depending entirely upon subsequent circumstances. The issue of Burgoyne's expedition was first to be known; and, besides, George might possibly be slain, or fall under the influence of some camp sickness. But, at all events, Caroline Mansfield was to become his wife, whenever the war closed, if he was permitted to return alive.

He pressed a warm parting kiss upon the lips of the lovely Caroline, and vaulting into his saddle, galloped away, with a light heart and a firm resolve, to win laurels upon the battle-field, that should entitle him to the respect of her father, or perish in the attempt.

Caroline watched his course, with a palpitating heart, until, descending a slope in the distance, he gradually disappeared from her sight. When his "nodding plume" could no longer be seen, she turned away and fell into a profound reverie, that was only broken by the return of her parents.

CHAPTER VII

Glanmore's band organized at the Cave—Assumes, with his band, the disguise of Indians—His cousin returns from his father's house—Having all things ready, they set out on their first Expedition—Mynheer Von Clump—His wife's garrulity betrays to the robbers the secret vault in which his money is secreted—Glanmore and his party attack his house, murder him and his wife, and carry off his money.

When Glanmore had collected his whole band at the cave, and got a sufficient quantity of provisions, arms, and ammunitions in store, the next consideration was, as to what disguise they should assume, in order not to be recognized, in the event of being met by any person while on their contemplated nightly expeditions.

It was finally agreed, to adopt the Indian dress. That would be a strong safeguard to them, for the inhabitants of the surrounding country would suppose that they were a band of predatory Indians, that had ventured out from the British army, and in case of pursuit, would never think of looking for them in the immediate neighborhood.

For a whole week after assembling at the cave, they were employed during the night, in enlarging their quarters, and digging the shaft extending to the root of the lofty hollow pine, that was to serve as a ventilator.

During this time, they slept during the day; but, sleeping days and working nights at subterraneous digging, ill comported with the views of these men. They had embarked in their wicked and murderous scheme with a view of wresting gold from those who might happen to possess it, without regard to any laws or rules of conduct, human or divine; and it was with the greatest difficulty that Glanmore could restrain them from making sorties against the neighboring Whig families, until the man who had been sent to his father's house with his horse, returned. He finally returned, and assured the gang, that the false news and letter he had carried, had succeeded to a charm in allaying all suspicions as to Glanmore's absence; and that they really believed him now, to be a prisoner within the British lines; and moreover, that Glanmore's father had pointed out to him the residence of an old Dutchman, who was supposed to have money hoarded in his house. It was forthwith decided, by the bandits, that an attempt should be made the next night upon the house of the old Dutchman.

Mynheer Von Clump was descended directly from the old New Netherlands stock, and by means of persevering industry, aided by his industrious *vrow*, had succeeded in clearing up a large farm in old Saratoga. Being free from debt, he converted his crops into hard cash, and hoarded it in his house with a miserly spirit; and if he ever bowed in devotional worship, it was when he kneeled down beside a large oaken chest, that contained a shining pile of dollars. This chest was concealed in a vault dug in the darkest corner of his cellar, a small room being partitioned off in that corner, and kept carefully locked, ostensibly for the purpose of securing sundry barrels of old whisky and cider, from the insidious attacks of his workmen; as well as to preserve his *vrow's* krout, sweetmeats and liverwort, from the attacks of rats; but really for the purpose of screening all eyes (except his own and those of his vrow) from the secret door, that led to the vault, directly underneath, where were deposited his hoarded and much beloved hard dollars. Never did Mynheer seat himself with greater satisfaction upon the rustic seat in front of his substantial log-house, than on the evening of the fifteenth of June, 1777. As the smoke ascended in curling clouds from his well-blackened pipe, he surveyed his broad fields, all covered with luxuriant grass and wheat; and as the twilight faded away, he recounted to his vrow, with evident delight, the excellent sale he had that day made, of a large quantity of oats, to an agent of the American army; and going into the house, counted over and over again the notches he had cut on a stick he kept for the purpose, denoting the number of dollars, the proceeds of his oats, that he had that day deposited in his oaken chest. But the hour for retiring drawing nigh, Mynheer cautiously fastened his doors—more cautiously now than formerly—first, because his workmen slept in their own houses, at some distance from his; and lastly, because his arm had lost much of its former strength and agility; and at this time, no man was sure, when he laid down at night, whether he might not be robbed and murdered before morning. After fastening his doors and windows—which last appurtenances gave him no great trouble, as they did not abound in very great profusion, in the log-cabins of the early settlers, he took a lighted candle, and went cautiously down into his cellar, through the locked door of the partitioned room, and down the dark steps of his vault. Opening the chest, he placed the candle in such a position as to display the shining pile in the bottom of the chest. He rubbed his hands in ecstacy, and ejaculated, "O! mien Got! vat a pig pile of tollars den!" But, alas! this was the last time, but one, that ever Mynheer was to look upon his "pig pile of tollars." He continued gazing upon his money for a few minutes, occasionally taking up a handful, and letting them drop back one by one, listening to the music they made, with as much delight, as any modern lover of music ever listened to the notes of the Swedish Nightingale.

Carefully locking the chest, and fastening all the doors about the cellar, he drew a mug of cider and returned to his capacious kitchen; when he and his vrow again filled their pipes, to indulge, for a few moments before retiring, in the luxury of "shmoking and trinking *cuyter* den."

The soothing influence of the "shmoke and cuyter" softened the hearts and unloosed the tongues of Mynheer and his wife.

"Mynheer," said Mrs. Von Clump, "if we should ever be so blest, as to git over dis plaguey war, den, mit de Englishmens"—

"Well, mien vrow, vat den?" said Mynheer.

"Vy, den," said Mrs. Von Clump, "ve vould pild a pig house, mit pig vinders, and paint it mit white all round."

"Vell, den," said Mynheer, "how you get money to pild such pig house mit?"

"Vy, I goes right down cellar, den, I turns the cuyter barrel round, I goes to the krout barrel, and turns him over the liverwust piggin, and I finds von little door, I turns dis little door over, and den I sees a pig chest, mit pig pile of tollars in. I goes right down into the chest, and unlocks him mit de pig key, dat carries himself in Mynheer Von Clump's pig pockit. I den takes out from de pig chest von thousand tollars, and more as dat, five hundred; and I sends Mynheer Von Clump away after the saw mill as makes de poards, and so I pilds von pig house.

"Vell, den," responded Mynheer, "If I know you pe sich a womans, I never marriet you, den, but I would go right off and marrit Ratrina Von Troukles."

While this interesting conversation was progressing between Von Clump and his amiable wife, a dark form, enveloped in an Indian blanket, was peering in upon them, through a cranny in the old log kitchen, overhearing every word that passed between them, and gaining a tolerable fair knowledge, from Mrs. Von Clump's description, of the exact location of the old Dutchman's money. Mynheer, having finished "shmoking" his pipe, took another cautious look all around at his doors and windows; and, finally, under the soothing influence of the "shmoke and cuyter," fell into a profound sleep, with his vrow;

he, to dream of huge piles of shining dollars—and *she*, of building a "pig house, mit pig windows, painted white all round, den." The dark form watched all the movements of Mynheer and his wife—and, after becoming satisfied that Mynheer was asleep, as he overheard him snoring luxuriantly, stole softly across a field adjoining Mynheer's house, on the north, and came to a dark piece of woodland. He uttered a low whistle, and was immediately surrounded by Gordon Glanmore and the balance of the band. He recited to his eager listeners all that he had overheard; and with high hopes of successful plunder, they stole softly across the field, and halted a few rods in the rear of Von Clump's house. As they stood silently listening, in order to be assured that no one was travelling along the road, or moving about the premises, Glanmore's heart began to fail him. What had poor old Von Clump ever done to him or his, that he should thus invade, with a band of robbers, his peaceable home at midnight? Nothing, most assuredly. But yet he had money! O, yes! he had enough—he believed him to be a Whig; and that was a sufficient excuse, in the estimation of a Tory, at that day, for the perpetration of the most revolting crime.

The band, all armed to the teeth, were now silently arranged about the house;—one was placed at each window and door; and the balance were stationed at the main door, not, however, without first trying the outside cellar-door, to find if it was not possible to reach the spot described by Mrs. Von Clump, without arousing the sleeping Von Clump, whose snoring could be distinctly heard; but Mynheer had fastened it too carefully. The main body then stepped back a few paces from the house, and one of them knocked loudly at the door. Von Clump started, awoke and listened;—the loud knock being repeated, he sprang from his bed and demanded "who was there?" He was answered "an *acquaintance*, who has come a long distance to see you, and got belated on the road." "Dunder and blitzen," whispered Von Clump to his wife, "I beliefs its some robber, as vants my monies." "Phew, Mynheer! you ish always tinking apout peing ropt," said Mrs. Von Clump; "light a candle den, and go along den and open de door."

Mynheer, however, first went to the window, and peering out into the darkness, could see nothing except a single form near the door; perceiving by the voice and language of the individual that he was an American, he took courage, and softly opened the door, intending to peer into the face of the stranger, and if his appearance did not suit him, to shut the door upon him. Mynheer had no sooner released the door from its fastenings, than five men, in Indian dress, sprang against it, and poor Mynheer was knocked flat upon the floor. He was instantly seized, and a handkerchief tied tightly over his mouth, and his arms pinioned by cords, with which the band were always provided. Mrs. Von Clump, frightened almost out of her senses, was commanded to get back into bed, and threatened, with a drawn sword pointed at her heart, that if she made any noise above her breath, they would run her through instantly; the poor old woman nestled down under the bedclothes; two men kept guard over her, while others ransacked the house, to discover if any other persons were in it. After having satisfactorily ascertained that no other persons were in the house but Von Clump and his wife, they called the balance of the gang, and placed one at each side of the house, and one at some distance each way on the road to keep a look-out. They next, after convincing Von Clump that they would murder him if he made any noise or resistance, took the bandage from his mouth, placed him in a chair, and with their drawn swords pointed towards him, demanded where his money was concealed.

"I tell you, *shentlemen* Injins, I has got no money."

The demand of the robbers being repeated, Von Clump invariably answered, "I tell you shentlemen Injins, I has got no money."

"There is no use of losing time in parleying with him," said one of the band; "for who ever saw an old Dutchman that would not sooner part with his life than his money."

"Come, old fellow," said Glanmore, "you shall pay for your obstinacy, for if you have any rusty dollars about here, you shall see us take them before your eyes."

So saying, they laid hold of the old man and hauled him along to the spot where his coat lay, and there in a secret pocket they found two keys. They then proceded to the cellar, taking Von Clump with them, unlocked the door, and searched for the "leetle door" mentioned by Mrs. Von Clump; at length, after removing an old krout barrel, and sundry other articles, they found a spot that emitted a hollow sound. Removing a few inches of dirt that was carefully packed over it, they discovered a trap-door, just large enough to admit the body of a large man to pass through. The key taken from Von Clump's pocket fitted the lock that confined it—they opened it and one of the gang descended. There was the chest spoken of by the old woman, the money must be here; how lucky, thought they, to find it so soon. The chest was opened, and lo! the shining dollars came forth. The robbers gloated over it—they scooped it out of the chest and threw it into a bag—they probed around in the earth, at the bottom of the vault—there might be other vaults—more money concealed there—but there was none—there stood five midnight robbers, painted and plumed to represent savages—savages that would disdain to commit such deeds for gold. And there too, stood Von Clump—he who had for long years been striving and toiling to collect that bag of dollars, now about to disappear from his possession for ever. He, who had prized that pile of dollars beyond anything on earth, or in heaven—yes, he stood there, and stared with a fixed unearthly gaze at that bag of dollars, and uttering a wild exclamation, fell down by the bag, grasping it with a death-like firmness, seeming determined, despite the efforts made by the robbers to release his grasp, to cling to it while life remained.

Finding that they could not release his hold, they consulted about what they should do with him;—one was for shooting him down in the vault; another was for killing him and burying him in the vault; but one of the oldest of the gang, stepping up to Glanmore, whispered in his ear, "You are our leader, you must set the example;—you know the motto, 'Dead men tell no tales.'"

Glanmore turned deadly pale, his hands, as yet, had never been stained by human blood; he hesitated to slay a fellow-creature in cold blood, but the rest of the gang calling loudly for the old man's life, he drew his tomahawk, and with one blow dashed out the unfortunate man's brains. Von Clump seeming lost to everything but his money, exhibited his "ruling passion strong in death," and continued his grasp even after the pulsations of his heart had ceased. They tore the bag from his grasp, all besmeared with the blood of their victim, and tumbled his body into the chest from which they had taken the money. When they were about to leave with their booty, perceiving that the blood fell in drops from the bag, they determined to procure another one for the money, and in the meantime concluded that it would be good policy to dispatch the old woman, and put her into the chest with the old man, as in all probability they were the only persons who knew of the existence of this subterraneous vault.

Two of the company were dispatched to assist those who guarded the old lady, in bringing her down; but this was unnecessary, for when they came to raise the bedclothes from her, they found the vital spark extinct. She, probably half dead with affright, being so snugly inclosed in the bedclothes, expired in consequence of the exhausted atmosphere in the closely confined bed, there not being sufficient air to re-invigorate her after she swooned. The old woman's "dying of her own accord," as the elated robbers called it, was a great relief to the gang. They packed her body into the chest along with her murdered husband, and shutting the lid tightly, and locking it, came out with the bag of money, carefully removing all blood from their hands and feet, so as to leave no stains about the house. They then closed the small trap-door, placed the dirt over it, and put the articles that were on it, in exactly the same position as they found them. They carried away the keys of the trap-door, and threw them into Saratoga lake—fastened the house, and made good their way back to their cave at Snake Hill, coming there just as the grey dawn was appearing in the East.

The next morning, when Von Clump's hands came to their accustomed work, they were surprised to find no one about the house. They supposed that perhaps the old gentleman and his wife had been summoned to attend the sick bed of one of their children, who lived at no great distance. Finally, discovering the horses were all in the field, and the wagon in its accustomed place, they became alarmed; and forcing open the door, searched all over the house for the old people. Failing to find them, they mounted the horses, and rode away to the old man's neighbors, and from thence to the several abodes of his children. The whole country, for miles around, was aroused, but no traces of Mynheer Von Clump and his wife could be found. The neighboring people were unanimously of the opinion that they had been robbed, murdered, and secreted by some one, but who had committed the deed, no one could tell. Von Clump's children themselves, were not aware of the existence of the secluded vault in their father's cellar; and, when the neighbors would have probed the cellar with a crowbar, to ascertain whether anything was secreted there, and if so, if it had recently been removed, they assured them that there was nothing in the rumors about their father having money buried in his cellar. The house was thoroughly searched, the country was scoured, but no traces of the old people were discovered until some years afterwards.

Von Clump's children, being thoroughly imbued with superstition, and always believing their father and mother to be a wizard and witch, and to have had dealings with the evil one, expressed the opinion confidently among themselves, that "den duyvel" had whisked the old people off. So strongly were they impregnated with this belief, that none of them would ever afterwards live in the house. The farm was sold; and, a few years after the Revolution, the proprietor, in endeavoring to erect a new house upon the old foundation, attempted to enlarge and deepen the cellar, when lo! the vault was discovered by him and his workmen. There, too, stood an old, oaken, mouldy chest. All the stories in relation to old Von Clump's money and hidden treasures, were recalled. With breathless haste and eager hands they broke open the chest, but, instead of gold or silver, two ghastly skeletons were revealed! The old inhabitants were of the opinion that the skeletons were those of Von Clump and his wife. The cellar was filled up, and the spot abandoned as a building site. Such are some of the strange revelations that were made after the close of the American Revolution!

CHAPTER VIII.

The Success of the Bandits inspires them with Confidence—Glanmore longs for an Opportunity of forwarding his Plans with regard to Miss Mansfield—Goes to his Father's House—Obtains the Perusal of a Letter from Rushwood—His Father entices an American Soldier into his House, and Murders him—Glendower discovers a Letter in the Murdered Man's Pocket, from Miss Mansfield to Rushwood.

The success of Glanmore and his band in the expedition against Von Clump, inspired them with confidence, and after dividing the money obtained from him, they began to cast about for new victims and new enterprises. During the succeeding summer, many Whigs fell victims to their midnight attacks—the most cold-blooded murders were perpetrated. The sleeping victims were aroused from their midnight slumbers. Men, women and children fell before them; and to recite the incidents where innocent and affrighted children were slaughtered while clinging to their mothers' bosoms—where old, decrepid men were left to wander away at midnight, by the light of their dwellings, to which the torch had been applied by these merciless tories, would be, but recounting deeds of a like nature with those that have been handed down to all the citizens of this country, who have from the pages of history, or from the lips of actors in the scenes of the American Revolution, learned the character of the acts committed by prowling bands of tories during that tremendous contest.

But these avocations did not satisfy Glanmore—he longed to be engaged in some plan for accomplishing the main purpose of his life. For although in nearly every expedition he made considerable addition to his stock of money, yet he accomplished nothing towards removing Rushwood from his path to the heart of Miss Mansfield.

Among his band was a cousin of his, in whom he placed the most implicit confidence, and to him he confided the secret of his heart. He listened with great attention to all Glanmore's plans for accomplishing his purpose. Finally it was agreed between them that he should go into the American army under St. Clair, where they learned that Rushwood was quartered, keep a strict watch upon his movements, and take his life the first opportunity that offered.

Before the young man took his departure, Glanmore secretly visited his father's house, and obtained the perusal of a letter that George Rushwood had sent by the hands of a soldier to his mother.

The old lady was so elated with hearing from her son, and so anxious that all those she considered her friends should participate in her joyous feelings, that she freely lent the letter to any of them who desired to see it; and that they all did, for any correct news from the army, was of the greatest and most absorbing interest to all at that time, whether Whigs or Tories, for Burgoyne was actually advancing and spreading death and desolation in his track. Little did she imagine, when old Glanmore sent a messenger to her house, requesting to borrow the letter she had received from her son, that his most deadly and inveterate enemy was lurking in Glanmore's house, and only wished to learn the contents of the letter, in order to find exactly where her son was located, that he might place a villain on his track, who would hunt him out and destroy him. The old lady did not hesitate to send her much-valued letter to her neighbor Glanmore, felicitating herself that he would be highly pleased with the success of her darling son. Gordon Glanmore read the letter with avidity. It ran thus:

AMERICAN CAMP, Aug. 25, 1777.

Dear Mother,—I embrace the present opportunity, the first that I have had since leaving home, to inform you of the state of my health, and of the prospects of the American army. But as you will be anxious to learn how I have fared, and what dangers I have passed through, I will endeavor to give you a brief account of the manner in which I have been employed since entering the army. You doubtless learned that our company were attached to the army under the command of Gen. St. Clair.

On the first of July, Burgoyne invested Ticonderoga, and St. Clair perceiving no safety but in flight, ordered a retreat. We retreated first into Vermont, and from thence to the Hudson River, where we joined General Schuyler's division. My company have been mainly employed in ranging the country for supplies, keeping a look-out on the movements of the enemy, and in tearing up bridges and felling trees, in order to impede his progress. Our first lieutenant having been killed in a rencontre with a British scouting party, I have received a commission in his stead. Our prospects are brightening: Gen. Stark, with a body of brave Green Mountain Boys, the other day attacked a body of five hundred English and one hundred Indians, near Bennington, and totally defeated them, with a loss on their part of three hundred killed and wounded, while the Americans lost but one hundred, This providential victory has raised the hopes and courage of our troops, and they long for nothing so much as to meet the whole body of the British army hand to hand, as they feel confident that the victory will be theirs.

General Schuyler has been superseded in the command by Gates, and I am strongly of the opinion that a general engagement between the two armies will soon take place. Fear not, dear mother; for although the thunder of British cannon may for awhile alarm you, as in the event of a general engagement it will probably be within your hearing, perhaps very near your hitherto peaceful home; yet, remember, that there are brave hearts and strong arms in the American army, and when they come to engage the enemy in sight of their own homes, they will, I know, be invincible. Victory will be theirs, and the hired minions of England will be driven far from their peaceful dwellings.

If we should defeat Burgoyne, I shall probably be at home with you this winter; if not, may God hold you safe within the hollow of his hand. My health has been good since I left home. I send this letter to you by the hands of a soldier who is on leave of absence to visit his sick wife. When he returns, which will be in a very few days, send me an answer by him, which I will instruct him to call for. If age has so far dimmed your sight, and enervated your hand, that you cannot well write, go over to Mr. Mansfield's and request Caroline to write for you. I know that she is too kind-hearted a girl to deny you such a request. It will afford me great pleasure to hear from you.

Your affectionate son,

George Rushwood.

Glanmore devoured with eagerness every word of this letter.

"So," he mentally exclaimed, "he does not write to Miss Mansfield directly, fearing, I suppose, that the letters might fall into the hands of her father; but he expects, that while she is writing for his mother, she will probably write something on her own separate account; perhaps that is the understanding between them. I must intercept that letter, and from it I shall probably learn how far matters have actually progressed between them."

He found, upon inquiries that he started while he lay concealed in his father's house, that the soldier would return, on his way to the American camp, in three days from that time. When the shades of night threw their sombre gloom over the surrounding country, he repaired to the cave, and informed his men that he wished four of them to go with him to his father's house immediately. They objected, alleging as a reason, that they might be captured there by some of the Whigs, who now aroused by the injuries, suffered by them in the course of the past summer, were scouring the country in every direction. Glanmore assured them that they were perfectly safe in his father's house, as no one suspected him of being anything but a thorough Whig. All their objections being silenced, they set out for the old Tory's house, and arrived there before the dawn of the morning.

Here they were concealed for two days. At length, on the morning of the third day, the soldier came in view, on his way to the American army. The old Tory went out and hailed him, making at the same time many inquiries touching the movements of the two armies, solemnly averring that he hoped and trusted that victory would ultimately crown the American army, and encircle the brows of the brave patriots with laurel wreaths, although, at the same time, he wished the American army annihilated and the British triumphant. He invited the soldier into his house, and offered him a glass of cider, alleging that it would invigorate him on a foggy September morning. He insisted upon the soldier's remaining until dinner-time, as he wished to write a letter to Gen. Schuyler, praying him to endeavor to effect, if possible, the exchange of his son Gordon, who was then, as he alleged, a prisoner of war at New-York, for some British soldiers, that he understood were shortly to be exchanged for American prisoners. The soldier consented to stay; and moreover being a jolly fellow, made extremely free with the old Tory's cider. The old man being perfectly acquainted witn his son's plan for intercepting the letter of Rushwood's mother, left the room, after placing another mug of cider at the disposal of the soldier, as he alleged for the purpose of looking up the materials for writing the letter to Schuyler. Going into the adjoining apartment, where his son was, he informed him that as the soldier seemed extremely fond of cider, he thought they might get possession of the letter, which the soldier informed him he had in his pocket, without intercepting him on the road, as had been proposed. Glanmore was well p.eased with the idea, as it would relieve him and his men of some fatigue and danger. The old man returned with the stationery, and commenced writing the letter; the garrulous soldier was furnished with pipe and tobacco, and amused himself by telling stories to the old Tory's wife, drinking a mug of cider whenever he had finished reciting some daring exploit of himself or his companions in arms. At length the old German clock, that stood in the corner of the room, with its tall head protruding above the main ceiling, into a hole that had been made there for its accommodation, struck eleven.

"Come friend," said the soldier, after ejecting a tremendous volume of smoke from his pipe, "it appears to me that you are writing an everlastin', almity long letter. See, it is eleven o'clock. If I am catched out after dark alone, I shall probably fare bad, if I fall into the hands of them cussed tory stragglers."

The old man appearing all absorbed by his letter-writing, made no reply, but the old woman, catching the hint, exclaimed—

"La! me! you don't think of going before dinner! You sartinly promised to eat dinner with us; and now, since it is so near twelve o'clock, we wouldn't consent to let you go without your dinner. We never allow any one who fights for liberty, to go away from our house hungry."

Her allusion to "fighting for liberty" had the effect she wished upon the soldier. She had touched him upon the right point.

"Wal," said he, "seein' your'e such a good Whig, I don't care if I do take some dinner with you, if you hurry up and get it ready soon."

She bustled around, and perceiving that the soldier had again drained the cider mug, did not forget, when she went into the cellar after some of her "nice fresh mutton chops," which, she took occasion to remark, "must taste first-rate to the palate of a war-worn soldier," to return it to him brimming full of sparkling cider; and as she supposed that his perception by this time was not remarkably acute, she mixed with it some old whiskey, in order that it might more speedily intoxicate him. The soldier either not perceiving the addition made to his beverage, or else relishing it all the better, made such havoc with the contents of the mug, that by the time the old woman had got her dinner nearly ready, it was drained to the dregs.

The soldier now began to show signs of deep intoxication, and settling himself back into his chair, he fell into a profound sleep.

The old man rubbed his hands, delighted with the success of his scheme. Repairing again to Glanmore's secret apartment, he informed him that now was the time for securing the letter. They had counted on the soldier's being so intoxicated that they could take the letter from his pocket, break it open, read, and return it, but in this they were mistaken. The soldier was not so far intoxicated, but that when the bandit chief approached him and thrust his hand into his pocket, he awoke, and apparently conscious of the treachery that was being practiced upon him, sprang up, and perceiving Gordon Glanmore, with whom he had formerly been acquainted, cried out with the voice of a stentor, "It is you, Gordon Glanmore! you are a Tory! you have got me in here to murder me."

Glanmore comprehended his danger in an instant. If the soldier escaped, he would be exposed—this must not be suffered to take place—and as the soldier was making rapidly towards the door, he drew a pistol and shot him dead on the spot. He fell with a dull heavy sound.

"We are ruined!" exclaimed the old Tory, "don't you see the workmen are coming to dinner!"

In an instant Glanmore caught up the body of the murdered soldier, and carried it into another room. He was gone, but there was blood on the floor!—the men were coming, they would yet be exposed, but as crime is ever fruitful in expedients, the old man caught up an axe that stood in the corner of the room, and gave the old house dog that was lying on the floor, a blow that nearly severed one of his feet from his leg. The old dog set up a tremendous yelling, and hobbled about the floor, besmearing it with blood from his wounded foot.

Just as the workmen arrived, the old woman was busily engaged in endeavoring to "do up the poor dog's foot," that she said "had been cut by one of their sharp axes, that they had carelessly left standing in the corner of the huge old-fashioned fire-place." She rated them soundly for leaving the axe there, and in order to appease her apparent wrath, they held the dog while she "done up his foot," and they promised her, moreover, not to be so negligent in future.

The murder having been so far concealed, the old Tory sat down and ate a hearty dinner, delighted with the piece of secret service he had accomplished for King George.

When dinner was over, and the workmen had returned to the distant corn-field, where they were engaged in "cutting up corn," the old woman commenced scouring out the blood stains from the floor, and the old man went into the room where his son sat like a statue, with the letter he had taken from the murdered soldier's pocket, in his hand.

"Come," said he, "don't sit there musing over that infernal letter, but stir about, and let's conceal this body before the farm hands come in at night."

The four concealed bandits were called—a consultation was held, in relation to the concealment of the body. What should they do with it? It would not be safe to carry it out until night, and even then, where could they conceal it without some-one's finding the grave eventually? "Sure bind is sure find," said the old Tory, wrapping the body in a blanket, and directing the men to carry it to the cellar; here he instructed them to take down a section of the cellar wall in a very dark corner.

After thus taking down the wall, they dug a hole directly back of it, sinking it beneath the foundation some feet—tumbled the dead soldier in, all wet with gore as he was, and again replaced the wall in such a manner, that the grave was never discovered, until the troubled conscience of the old Tory caused him to reveal the whole transaction on his death-bed.

After the body was concealed and the shades of night had once more closed o'er the landscape, Glanmore, with his four followers made their way back to the cave, at Snake Hill; he was deeply disappointed with the issue of the plan for obtaining a perusal of the letter. After his men were sunk in sleep, he sat down on a rude seat in his dark cave, and read over and again, the portion of the letter that Miss Mansfield had added, as he before expressed it, "on her own account." It read as follows:—

Dear George,—Having finished writing for your mother, I take the liberty of filling the balance of the sheet, in order to assure you that my sentiments towards you remain unchanged, I might perhaps say strengthened, as the reports of your gallant and generous conduct, on several occasions, while engaged with the enemy, have more than confirmed my former high opinion of you.

I perceive by the reports from the army, that your gallantry has been rewarded by a lieutenant's commission. Although you evidently suppose, judging from your letter to your mother, that we hear nothing from you, yet in this you are mistaken. There are a great number of sick and disabled soldiers calling at our house, on their return from the army, and without a single exception, all who know you as a soldier and an officer, speak in the highest terms of you. These good reports in regard to you have made a decidedly favorable impression on my father's mind; and if you continue to thus add laurels to your brow, every impediment to our union will be entirely removed, for during these exciting times father and mother have grown exceedingly patriotic—so much so, that they look upon a scar, or a good gallant name, won in defence of our suffering and bleeding country, as a badge of true nobility. So press on manfully, heroically, my dear George; and may the God of battles preserve you unharmed, and may you be enabled soon to return victorious to the home of your youth, there to repose upon the laurels you have so nobly won.

Yours truly,

CAROLINE MANSFIELD.

P. S. I almost forgot to tell you that since you left for the army, we have heard from Gordon Glanmore. He has written a very pathetic letter to his father, in which he states that he is well used by the British who hold him prisoner. This is certainly remarkable; for if he is well used, he is assuredly an exception to other American prisoners. It confirms your suspicions in my mind. But if he is really a prisoner, and so well used, I hope, for our sakes, they will continue to keep him and use him well, until you defeat Burgoyne, and our hopes are consummated. I commend your prudence in not writing to me, as it might arouse a feeling in father's bosom, unfriendly to our prospects.

C. M.

"Ah!" mentally exclaimed Glanmore, after reading this postscript; "then they are really betrothed. But"—and he paused, with clenched teeth—"but—they—never shall—be married—while I live. I will hunt him down—I will pounce upon him—even as the fierce and bloodthirsty panther pounces upon his prey. Oh! that I could have read this letter! and then that he could have read it! and as his heart beat high with hope, I could have plunged a dagger into it, and as his life-blood oozed away, I could have tauntingly repeated to him the knowledge I possessed—then my revenge would have been complete. But," and he arose and paced the cave with hurried strides, "he shall read it, and he shall then die! Yes! this shall take place, even if I have to carry it to him myself, and perish in the attempt."

CHAPTER IX.

Glanmore's Reflections—Discovers an Indian fishing near his Cave—Builds a Canoe—Sends an Emissary into the American Camp.

Those who understand the deep inworkings of the human heart, cannot fail to appreciate the feelings of our hero at this moment. The pent-up atmosphere of the cave seemed too close to sustain life; involuntarily he sought the invigorating atmosphere without the cave. He passed through the dark narrow passage leading out of the cave—he reached the open air. The stars looked down upon him through the overhanging canopy of thick foliage, an invigorating breeze came gently over the bosom of Saratoga Lake. It fanned his heated brow, and cooled his feverish brain. He cautiously made his way along the steep side of the hill, and coming to the trunk of a fallen and decaying tree, he seated himself upon it, and listened to the wild dull sound of the waves, as they beat in regular succession against the shore; for although Saratoga Lake is but a small sheet of water, yet it is a miniature Euxine, and a slight breeze is sufficient to raise a long rolling swell, that is truly astonishing to behold, considering the small area that its waters cover.

These soothing influences calmed the troubled waters of his spirit, and then conscience, that inward monitor, that works in the bosom many times, of the most depraved, spoke to him in slight, yet distinct accents; and as he looked back upon the last few months of his life, all blackened and stained with revolting crimes, his spirit sunk within him, and he viewed with deep and poignant anguish the yawning chasm that now separated him from his former innocence: Ah! he would fain at that moment have retraced those steps, but a mountain barrier, towering like the lofty Alps, seemed to rise between him and his former innocence. He possessed not the moral courage to sustain him in this trying moment—but hark! he listens, his quick and ever watching ear detects a sound! a sound that he had not before heard upon the lake since he had made his dark abode there; he listens again, it must be the light dipping of an oar, it struck upon his ear at regular intervals, there could be no mistaking it. He bent forward and looked out upon the lake in the direction of the sound. He could perceive an object at some distance, for the grey dawn of the morning was fast approaching. At length he beheld a small dark object in the distance—gradually it neared him. It was the light birchen canoe of an Indian, and as it was propelled by the stalwart arm of its only occupant, it danced lightly and buoyantly over the long rolling swells of the lake; but in his eagerness he forgot that he had exposed himself to the keen, far-seeing eye of an Indian. However, he might not have seen him—so thought Glanmore. Rolling his body cautiously over the log, and lying down behind it, he found that it would effectually screen him from view; and as there was a crook in it that raised it from the ground, it afforded him a convenient lookout from beneath.

The canoe came within a few rods of the shore. He saw the Indian take a rude anchor and drop it into the water, and then, with his fishing tackle in his hand, seat himself quietly in his canoe. He saw the Indian bring up with dexterous hand one after another of the piscatory tribe: beautiful yellow perch; elastic pickerel; and huge sunfish brought he forth. Apparently much absorbed in the sport, he did not relax his efforts until the sun had mounted high in the heavens. Glanmore scanned the dark features of the Indian—he knew him now: yes, it was Kwa-ta-hu, an eccentric old Indian, that had many times visited his father's house. A thought struck him—could he not bring this Indian into his service, and make of him an instrument for the destruction of his rival in love? But then he recollected that this Indian was in the habit of visiting Mr. Mansfield's house also, and that once, when wounded near there, while hunting, by the bursting of his rifle, George Rushwood, attracted by the sound, had discovered him lying senseless upon the ground; that through Rushwood's efforts, he had been carried to Mansfield's house; and that while confined there by his wounds, Caroline Mansfield had ministered to his necessities with her own hands. No, he could not, in view of these things, make an instrument of him to carry out his dark designs. There was too much of gratitude, too much of nobleness, in the nature, even of this savage, wild and untutored as he was, to be guilty of such an outrage, of such base ingratitude,—no, this Indian must not recognize him, not even see him, or all his prospects would be blasted, and his plans frustrated. Moved by these reflections to adopt the most extreme caution, lest he should be discovered and recognized by the very being that he had fancied but a moment before, might be of great and essential benefit to him, he lay there beneath the trunk of the decayed tree trembling. Why did he thus tremble, dear reader?

Because crime, ever conscious of its own enormity, shuns the open gaze of the world, and shrinks from the most insignificant of God's creatures, that it supposes may in any way bring its dark deeds to light.

When the old Indian had finished fishing, he paddled his canoe to the shore, drew it up on a sand-bar, and came directly up the hill towards our hero. "Can it be possible," thought Glanmore, "that Kwa-ta-hu has discovered me? If so, he must die!" Cautiously examining the priming of his pistol, he cocked it, and lay ready to shoot Kwa-ta-hu the moment he should approach him. But Kwa-ta-hu was intent upon other business. He peered anxiously about upon the ground, and with a long forked stick carefully overturned every bunch of decayed foliage. Glanmore recollected now that Kwa-ta-hu was in the yearly habit of hunting rattlesnakes for their oil, which was held in high repute by many persons at this time, and indeed is now, for medicinal purposes. Glanmore heard the Indian utter the deep guttural Ugh! of the savage, and saw a monster snake glide away before him, and make directly up the hill towards the log behind which he lay. Kwa-ta-hu pursued it hotly. "The snake will take refuge under the fallen trunk, and I shall be discovered," mentally exclaimed Glanmore. He grasped his pistol more firmly; but Kwa-ta-hu was too quick and rapid in his movements for the snake. He made a pass at it, and fastened it to the ground with his forked stick. The snake struggled and writhed, and wound his supple body about the stick; and as Kwa-ta-hu held him fast, he uttered a low guttural laugh, evidently over the struggles of his victim. The snake finally partly worked itself out from beneath the stick. Kwa-ta-hu, fearful that the snake might bite its own body during its convulsive struggles, and thus infuse its poisonous virus through its oil, and render it worthless, relaxed his hold upon it, and suffered it to glide away, in order once more to get his stick firmly upon its scaly neck.

Glanmore expected to see the snake make again for the log; but instead of that, it leaped revengefully at the Indian, who anticipating its movement, struck it with his stick, and threw it far down the hill-side. Following up his advantage, Kwa-ta-hu, by another well-directed blow, ended the life of the hissing and poisonous serpent. Carefully suspending it upon his stick, he made good his way to the canoe, and as the sun had now well-nigh reached the meridian, soon paddled to the opposite shore of the lake.

Glanmore now breathed easier. His breath, that had before been drawn between his tightly clenched teeth, soon came and went freely. Hurrying to the cave, he related to the bandits the narrow chance he had run of being discovered. "I am, however, rather pleased with the adventure," said he, " as now we can guard ourselves against the searching eye of this savage. We must now plan out some way of reaching the cave in order to avoid his discovering our tracks, as the keen eye of an Indian would discover them where they would not be visible to a white man."

To this end they determined to build a canoe, capable of carrying the whole party, and by sinking the mouth of the passage to the cave, so that the water would flow into the outlet, they could run the canoe directly into it, entirely out of sight, as the entrance to the cave extended some eighty feet before it reached the main room. By using this canoe as a means of egress and ingress, they could obviate the difficulty entirely, and avoid making any tracks in the immediate vicinity of the cave—the hemlocks, pines, and thick intervening vines would entirely conceal, as they now did, the mouth of the cave.

Glanmore sent his men up the lake, where they felled a lofty pine, out of which they hollowed and shaped the proposed canoe. But he had another work to perform. He retained his cousin at the cave, and after the balance of the group were gone, instructed him in regard to the mission he had resolved to entrust him with. He directed him to depart that night, and make his way to old Glanmore's house. He must take the letter that had been obtained from the murdered soldier with him. He must there pretend to every one but the old tory that he was from the backwoods, and that he was on his way to the American army. He must pretend to purchase the powerful horse, supposed by his father's neighbors to have been brought back from Westchester. He must go into the American camp, and offer himself as a volunteer, under a fictitious name. The first favorable opportunity that offered, he must give the letter to George Rushwood, alleging to him, that as he had stopped on his way to purchase a horse in George's old neighborhood, his mother, hearing of his being there, had entrusted the letter to his care; that she had kept it some days, expecting to send it by the hands of a soldier who had brought her one, but that he had not yet returned. He must thereafter keep a strict watch upon the movements of Rushwood, and kill him the first opportunity that offered; after which he must fly, and make the best of his way back to the cave. If he performed this mission, he was to receive as a reward for his services the sum of two thousand dollars.

Night at length came, and all their plans having been mutually agreed to, Glanmore's cousin set out on his mission of blood.

In less than one week from this time he was within the American camp, where he was gladly welcomed, and attached to a company of cavalry.

CHAPTER X.

Rushwood returns Home on a Furlough—Visits Caroline Mansfield—Is waylaid by Glanmore, and comes near being Shot—Is Preserved by an unknown Hand—Fired at on his Return by the Bandits—Escapes Uninjured, and arrives Safely in the American Camp.

On the same night that Glanmore's emissary reached the American camp, a tall manly figure was seen approaching the neighborhood of Mr. Mansfield's residence. He was mounted upon a powerful and spirited horse, that came thundering along upon a rapid gallop: he was enveloped in the uniform of an American ranger, and seemed to sit impatiently upon his saddle, as if eager to reach his destination.

The evening was warm and sultry, and his foaming steed told that he had ridden far, and at a rapid rate. He did not halt at Mansfield's house; he cast a side-glance at the cheerfully lighted windows, as if expecting to behold some familiar image. He passed rapidly along until he came nearly to the residence of Widow Rushwood; he then slackened his pace, and brought his noble steed down to a slow walk; but the horse seemed loth to continue long upon this gait; he curvetted impatiently, pricked up his ears as if recognizing surrounding objects, and ambling sideways up to the Widow Rushwood's gate, gave utterance to a loud neigh. Yes! the war horse that had carried his brave rider through the thunder and crash of battle, seemed impatient to be again turned free, to roam through the green pastures of his early home.

Mrs. Rushwood started from her arm-chair, when the horse neighed, and exclaimed aloud, "That was Pompey's whinner, I could swear to it among a hundred horses."

It was indeed, as Mrs. Rushwood expressed it, "Pompey's whinner." Yes! George had come home, and as his aged mother went out of the house to meet him, he folded her to his bosom, and exclaimed: "My dear, dear mother! I have come back to you once more, safe and sound."

The old lady's heart was too full for utterance; she fainted in his arms, and was borne by the strong arms of her son into the house, where she speedily returned to consciousness.

When she recovered from her swoon, George unbuckled his sword, and threw it down upon a chair, exclaiming, "There, mother, is the sword you gave me, I trust I have not dishonored it."

"If the accounts I hear of you are true," said his mother, "you have not only done honor to your father's name, but have worn his sword like a brave, true-hearted son."

"Then you have heard from me!" said George.

"Yes, George, frequently," returned his mother; "there has been a number of sick and disabled soldiers passing along, some of them, poor fellows, begging their way back from the army to their homes; I hope, George, that they may receive their reward, if not in this world, in the world to come."

"Did you receive a letter from me, by the hands of a soldier?" said George.

"O! yes," continued his mother, "and dear Caroline Mansfield wrote one in return for me; she is a dear good soul. After she had finished writing for me, she said she would fill the sheet with a few words of her own, that might possibly help to cheer you on in your struggle for liberty. I guess she thinks a good deal of you, for while she was writing, the tears ran down her beautiful cheeks until they almost blinded her."

"But the letter, mother; I have not received it."

"You hav'nt! why I sent it by the soldier that brought yours; he came back a few days after he left your letter with me, and staid here all night; he went away early in the morning. He was so much afraid of losing the letter that he pinned it fast in his pocket."

"This is strange," said Rushwood; "the soldier has certainly not returned to the American camp, for I have been every day to his quarters, and the commanding officer of his company assured me that he had not returned."

"Poor fellow," said the old lady, "you may depend upon it he has fallen into the hands of the Tories. They have made dreadful work around here this summer. I expect every night when I go to bed, to be murdered before morning."

"Never mind, mother," said George, "their game will soon be up, in this region. In a few days we shall meet Burgoyne, and I do confidently believe we shall defeat him, and either take his army prisoners, or drive them back to Canada; I shall then get discharged, as the campaign will be ended, for this year, at least in the north; and as they will not wish to keep a large force in arms during the winter, I shall return home with some of my brave fellows, and we will hunt these tories down, and break up their rendezvous, for I am confident, in my opinion, that they have a nestling place somewhere about here. I wish old Kua-ta-hu would come along here now, I would set him at work to hunt out their hiding-place, for there is no one who knows so much about bye-places in the country."

"I have not seen Kua-ta-hu this summer," said his mother. "I was thinking, a few days ago, that it was strange he did not come along; he used every year to come about this time, with such lovely fish."

"Kua-ta-hu will turn up some of these fine mornings," said George, "and I expect to make him of service to me."

"Maybe he has gone over to the British," said the old lady.

"No fear of that," said George; "he has pledged his word to me, never to take up the hatchet against the Americans; he will never forfeit his word to me, for you know he thinks I saved his life when his rifle bursted. No, I have no fear of Kua-ta-hu; if I could leave you a protector against the attacks of the Tories, I would as soon trust Kua-ta-hu as any man I know of."

"How soon do you expect to return to the army, George?" said Mrs. Rushwood.

"I have a furlough for only a few days," returned George. "My anxiety to hear from you increased hourly. After the expiration of the furlough of the soldier who was to have brought me a letter from you, I went to Gates, and informed him of your situation, and he agreed to let me come home for a brief period. I wished to say farewell to you once more! to once more offer you the consolation of beholding your only child. In a very few days we shall meet Burgoyne's army in fearful conflict. Many of the youth in the army whose hearts now beat high with hope, will probably, nay must, fall in the terrible struggle. I may fall among that number, or I may not; but at all events, I have returned home to advise you what to do, in case I am slain in battle."—But we need not follow out the conversation of this happy mother and son, for they were happy; notwithstanding the darkness and uncertainty of the prospect before them, they were indeed supremely happy in again beholding each other. The son happy to find that his mother had escaped the scourge of the merciless Tories, and the mother happy that her son had returned unscathed, after passing through so many dangers. We need not tell our readers how they knelt that night around the family altar, or how that aged mother invoked the God of battles to guard and protect her beloved son through the terrible calamities of war, and to return him once more to the arms of his aged, and now almost helpless parent.

Next morning Rushwood set out for Mr. Mansfield's. No one in the neighborhood, as yet, knew that he had returned

That was known only to his mother. When he came near Mansfield's house he met the old gentleman, who received him in the warmest and most cordial manner; he led George into the house with a sort of triumph, proud that one in whom he had taken such a great interest, should have acquitted himself so nobly in arms. In a half-joking manner, he introduced George as Lieut. Rushwood; they received him with cordial greetings, but Caroline was too cautious, as yet, to disclose the deep thrilling emotions of her heart. Could she have been permitted to have acted out freely her own sentiments and feelings at that time, we should certainly have been obliged, in this place, to have recorded one of those tender, touching scenes that are generally attached to lovers' meetings, after having been so long absent from each other, under circumstances such as these; but prudence forbade such a course, as she was not yet clearly and fully persuaded that her parents would be willing to look with favor upon Lieutenant Rushwood as their future son-in-law.

Mr. Mansfield detained George until long after dinner, eagerly listening to his accounts of the campaign, and in return, giving him a history of the inroads and outrages of the Tories and Indians; indeed so much did the old gentleman engross the attention of his visitor, that he scarcely had an opportunity of conversing with Caroline at all. However, after a while, the old gentleman recollected that he had made an engagement to meet a neighbor on some business; excusing himself, therefore, for a half-hour, he took his hat and cane, and hurried away to meet his engagement.

The two lovers, perceiving that Mrs. Mansfield had retired to take her usual afternoon siesta, began to converse upon those things that more immediately interested them.

"Did you receive a letter from your mother, a few days ago, by the hands of a soldier?" said Caroline.

"I am sorry to say," replied Rushwood, "that I did not receive that letter, and that I fear the soldier who was to have delivered it to me, has been foully dealt with by some lurking foe."

"'Tis strange," said Caroline, thoughtfully; "but never mind," continued she, assuming a more cheerful countenance, "I can now tell you the contents, as I was the author of part of it myself, and had the balance dictated to me by your mother, while I acted in the capacity of amanuensis."

Knowing that his time was limited, George informed Miss Mansfield "that, as he must return to the army the next morning, it would afford him great pleasure if he could have a private interview with her that evening;" for, continued he,

"I perceive that your father is already coming; he must have dispatched his business quite hastily, or else the time has flown more rapidly than it generally does."

With that blindness to the passage of time that ever besets lovers, a half-hour had passed since Mr. Mansfield's departure. Reader, dost think it strange that so short a conversation as we have related, should have consumed so much precious time? But perhaps you are not yet aware, that after Mr. Mansfield's departure, and these two loving hearts found themselves alone, Rushwood took a seat beside the fair Caroline—that he pressed that fair and delicate hand—that he—shall I tell it, dear reader? —that he not only pressed that hand, but that—

"He stole the nectar from that lip,
A place where bees might love to sip."

And that then, for some moments, neither spoke, yet

'There was speech in their dumbness.
Language in their very gesture."

Each one of them could have said to the other,

"You have bereft me of all words,
Only my blood speaks to you in my veins;
And there is such confusion in my powers,
As after some oration fairly spoke
By a beloved prince, there doth appear
Among the buzzing, pleased multitude,
Where every something, being blent together,
Turns to a wild of nothing, save of joy,
Expressed, and not expressed."

Mr. Mansfield's footsteps approached the door, George snatched a hasty kiss, and whispering in the ear of his beloved a renewal of the request he had made, she answered: "I will meet you at the arbor, in the garden, at nine."

Lieutenant Rushwood was too good a soldier not to have learned that "discretion is the better part of valor," and accordingly beat a hasty retreat to the other side of the room, where he was quietly seated when Mr. Mansfield entered. That gentleman, versed in the knowledge of human nature, perceived that the young couple were a little confused, and calling to mind some former expressions made by Rushwood, and some little scenes that he had accidentally witnessed, could have truthfully said, in the language of the great philosopher of poets—

"He says he loves my daughter!
I think so too, for never gazed the moon
Upon the water, as he'll stand, and read
As 'twere my daughter's eyes. And to be plain,
I think there is not half a kiss to choose
Who loves another best."

He felt, too, that he had been guilty of a great indiscretion, in thus leaving them to renew that flame that he wished to smother; but to be plain about it, his admiration for Rushwood's brilliant career as a patriotic soldier, had in a great degree blinded his eyes to those defects and objections that had hitherto warped his mind against him, as ever standing in a nearer relation to him than that of a friend and protege. Still those objections existed, and still he looked forward to the union of his daughter with Glanmore, and consoled himself with the idea that she, knowing his aversion to Rushwood in a matrimonial sense, would not, as a dutiful child, encourage his addresses.

Soon after, Rushwood took his departure. Lightly, now, bounded that grateful heart of his. Caroline Mansfield, the idol of his life—she whose form had ever been present in his imagination, even while encountering the fierce hosts of Britain—was still true to him. The inward misgivings that would occasionally haunt him, were now all dispelled. These blissful thoughts soon gave way to those of a more gloomy nature. The bright ray of sunshine that had fallen upon his pathway during the last hour, must soon be dispelled by a return to scenes of blood, of strife, and terrible carnage. True, he might win laurels, a grateful posterity might write his name upon the page of history, and revere his memory as one of a brave band of men, who had met, fought and conquered those boasting invaders, who would otherwise have ground them beneath the iron heel of despotism. But what was all this to him, in his present frame of mind? He could truthfully exclaim with the poet—

" Give me the boon of love,
  I ask no more for fame;
For better one unpurchased heart,
  Than glory's proudest name.
Why wake a fever in the blood,
  Or damp the spirit now,
To gain a wreath whose leaves shall wave
  Above a withered brow.

" Give me the boon of love!
  Ambition's meed is vain;
Dearer affection's earnest smile,
  Than honor's richest train.
I'd rather lean upon a breast
  Responsive to my own,
Than sit pavilion'd gorgeously
  Upon a kingly throne.

" Give me the boon of love!
  Fame's trumpet-strains depart,
But love's sweet lute yields melody
  That lingers in the heart.
And the scroll of fame will burn,
  When sea and earth consume,
But the rose of love, in a happier sphere,
  Will live in deathless bloom!"

The full moon arose with that peculiar glow that characterizes its appearance in Autumn. Long shadows were thrown over the meadows, and the thickly standing and blackened stumps, that were still firmly rooted in many of the fields of the pioneers of the forest, revealed partially by moonlight, appeared like human figures rising up to view; and as one gazed upon them, while thus revealed "by the moon's pale light," it was easy enough, when aided by the imagination, to convert them into human figures; and again, it was just about as easy for any one that might be moving along among them, to convert himself into a stump in the imagination of any one who might get a glimpse of his movements, for if he supposed himself to be seen by any one at a distance, he could very easily convince them, especially if not over skeptical, that they were in error about his being a moving object, by standing perfectly still for a few moments. The early settlers were not over particular about cutting their timber so as to make the most of it; and as the clearing was generally done in the Winter, when the snow was deep, many of the stumps were as high as an ordinary man.

As Lieutenant Rushwood moved along towards Mr. Mans field's house, for the purpose of meeting his betrothed, earlier than was necessary, of course,

"As lovers ever run before the clock,"

he imagined that he saw, moving along in an adjacent field, a human figure, that nearly kept pace with him, and at some distance behind that, another figure, keeping pace with the first. He paused, and looked earnestly at the figures for some moments. They now stood still also. He continued to look steadfastly in the direction of the figures, until they appeared to him, through the haze of the evening, just like the blackened stumps that rose up in various parts of the field.

"I must be deceived," thought he; "it is my imagination that has converted the tall stumps into human beings." Again he went forward—again the figures moved; again he paused—again no figures could be seen moving.

"It is all a delusion," muttered he; "I have been so long accustomed to look out for prowling Indians and Tories, that my imagination converts every stump and bush I see after dark, into an Indian or a tory." But he was soon relieved from all uneasiness in regard to the forms he supposed he had discovered keeping pace with him in a suspicious manner. A dark cloud, that had been for some time looming up in the west, and gradually spreading itself across the heavens, at length veiled the moon, and by the low muttering thunder, far to the westward, he was convinced that a heavy and terrific thunder-storm would soon be upon him. He hurried along with rapid steps, forgetting that his suspicions had been aroused by the supposed moving forms. When he arrived near Mansfield's house, he paused. His noble nature flinched beneath the idea that he must grope around into the garden in a stealthy manner, for the mere privilege of a few brief moment's conversation with the object of his heart's affections. His lofty and daring spirit, aroused as it was, by a proud consciousness of his own deserts, hesitated, but nevertheless, being disposed to "take all the swift advantage of the hours," and recollecting that he had proposed the meeting himself, he quietly walked into the garden; and as the lightning flash fell upon the face of his watch, he perceived that it wanted a few minutes of nine o'clock. Had he looked in the right direction, at this time, he would have seen revealed by the glare of the lightning, a human figure, enveloped in an Indian costume, carefully stealing along among a clump of pines, that stood just back of the garden, and placing itself behind the body of one of the trees, peer out at him, as he stood waiting for the appearance of Caroline, having a fair view of him every time the lightning flashed athwart the heavens. And just in the rear of this figure, he would have discovered another, apparently watching the movements of the first, with even if possible, a greater degree of solicitude, that the first figure regarded those of Rushwood.

At length, a light appeared in the back window of the hall, and soon the door opened, and its light fell full upon the form of Rushwood.

"I am here," he said in a low tone, as the form of Caroline appeared.

"I am a few minutes behind the time," said Caroline; "the approaching thunder storm deterred my mother from retiring at her usual hour; not wishing to come out before she was asleep, I waited until she had retired."

"I will not detain you long out here, my dear Carry," said Rushwood; "at such a forbidding time as this. I wished to say a few more words to you before I went back to the army, as in a few days I expect to be engaged in a terrible battle with the enemy."

As they said these words, they walked on, arm in arm, down the garden path, the lightning momentarily revealing their forms and attitude to the fiendish glare of the first figure.

Their voices were low, but yet distinct; one who was not particularly interested in their conversation, listening to them, would have exclaimed with the poet,

> "How silver-sweet sound lovers' tongues at night,
> Like softest music to attending ears."

"Shall we take a seat here in the arbor?" said Rushwood.

"I would prefer standing at a little distance from the arbor," said Caroline, "that tree that stands just at the back of it may attract the lightning."

They halted, and with that deep earnestness that characterizes lovers that have been long separated, talked of their present plans and future prospects, all brilliant with hope, if George passed unscathed through the hard struggle for liberty, in which he was engaged; and, at the same time, scathed, withered, and blasted, if he fell upon the gory battle-field. Ah! little did they know that the glaring eyes, and listening ears of a terrible foe, were then within a few feet of them: no! they thought not now of lurking and unseen dangers; those hearts were now all the world to each other; they heeded not the appalling thunder that rolled overhead, nor the terrific lightning that played around them.

The rain began to fall in large and occasional drops. The first figure muttered something between his set teeth: he leaned eagerly forward to catch their low words. The second figure observing that the first was all-absorbed in listening to the young couple, moved very close to him; his warm breath could almost have been felt playing upon the neck of the first figure.

"The rain begins to fall," said Lieut. Rushwood, "we must part now, for if we stay here for hours, parting will be the same as now." So saying, he imprinted a farewell kiss upon her lips. The lightning revealed the scene to the first figure, and to him, the slight sound of those lips seemed louder than thunder, for dear reader, that figure was nothing more or less than the form of Gordon Glanmore, the bandit chief.

Glanmore drew a pistol from his girdle; the lightning seemed to play over the polished barrel in a bluish flame, and as he grasped a shining tomahawk in the other hand, he looked the very personification of a horrible savage, ready to pounce upon his victim.

"I have sworn it," muttered he,—the figure behind him heard the expression,—"yes! I will now be avenged!" continued he, in the same tone, "she shall see him die!"

Just at that moment, the lovers took the first step forwards towards the house, Glanmore was about to level his pistol with deadly aim, a terrific thunder-clap burst upon the scene, and as it came, the figure behind Glanmore dealt him a blow with the head of his tomahawk, that felled him to the ground, and prevented his firing the pistol. The terrific thunder-clap stunned the ears of the lovers so, that they heeded not the sound of the blow received by the bandit chief, nor did they hear the dull, heavy sound of his body, as he fell to the ground. They passed up the walk with rapid steps, and then they parted, with that lothness that is perfectly natural upon such occasions. Reader, wouldst thou know who the second figure was; who it was that dealt the providential blow that prevented the murderous ball from the bandit's pistol from entering the heart of George Rushwood? You shall know in due season.

Rushwood hurried homeward, unconscious of the narrow chance he had run of being murdered.

Next morning, at early dawn, he mounted his steed, and rode away, with a heavy heart, towards the American camp. Halting at Mansfield's, he bid them a hasty adieu, and touching his noble horse lightly with his spurs, dashed on impetuously for three miles before he checked his headlong course. He was just then entering a heavy tract of woodland; the road led straight through it, and the distant opening appeared like a small door, leading towards the rising sun.

When about half-way through the wood, his horse suddenly started with affright; looking around, he saw several Indians, painted and plumed, standing partially concealed behind trees, with their long rifles bearing directly upon him. Death stared him fully in the face. With a nervous effort, he plunged his spurs deeply into his horse. The horse bounded fearfully into the air, threatening to precipitate his rider from his back, as he swerved to one side of the road. The sharp crack of the rifles reverberated through the woods, and although the balls whistled around our hero, yet he escaped with the loss only of a part of the hair of his right ear-lock. His noble war horse bore him onward like the wind, and ere his enemies could reload their discharged rifles, he was out of their reach. When he arrived within a short distance of the American camp, the heavy roll of drums beating to arms, could be distinctly heard, and when fully arrived at the camp, he found the army in motion, preparing for a fearful and bloody encounter with the forces of Gen. Burgoyne.

CHAPTER XI.

Kua-ta-hu discovers the Bandit's Cave—Overhears their plans and plots against Rushwood—Kua-ta-hu is bitten by a snake —Cures himself by drinking the waters of the Hight Rock Spring.

After Kua-ta-hu had been discovered by the bandit chief, they enlarged the opening of the cave, and sunk it, so as to admit the canoe to glide in entirely out of sight. Whenever they went out after this, they did so in the night, and by means of the canoe; usually rowing to the nearest point, to such place as they wished to reach, and then concealing the canoe till they returned.

Kua-ta-hu now began to visit the lake daily, as it was now his time to catch bass, which he cured by smoking them for his winter's food; and it was also an excellent season for catching rattlesnakes, as they now began to gather together at the hill, where they laid up during the winter, in dens. He was a great source of annoyance to the band. They several times urged the propriety of taking his life, but as they were generally weary during the day, after their nightly expeditions, they deferred this necessary precaution, from time to time.

Kua-ta-hu was also in the habit of hunting, at this season of the year, for wild honey, that he sold readily to the white families about the country; and while he looked cautiously upon the ground for rattlesnakes, he also kept a sharp look-out among the old trees, to discover if any honey-bees were going in and out of the holes in them.

One day, while thus employed on Snake Hill, he came to the tall pine, that stood above the bandits' cave. Looking away up into the lofty top, he discovered the incisions that had been made by the bandits, to let the foul air of the cave escape. Again and again, he looked up at the holes, and then with instinctive curiosity, he looked on the ground for the chips that must have fallen from them, as he plainly saw that they had not been made any great length of time, but he could find none. This was singular; there was some mystery lurking here, else why should the chips have been gathered up and taken away so carefully ? He continued looking cautiously all around upon the ground, with the sharp and peculiar vision of his race. Not yet satisfied, he went up the hill, continuing his curious search, and then down to the very verge of the lake. Carefully pursuing his course along the shore, among the underbrush, and park evergreens, he at length discovered the passage leading into the cave. By sounding, he found the water that backed into it, to be but about three feet deep. He peered into the dark hole, and thinking that it had something to do with the incisions in the tree, determined to explore it. Stepping cautiously into the water, he waded along until he came to a bank of dirt, nearly as high as his head. He climed up the bank, and groped cautiously along, feeling the width of the entrance on each side, and carefully sounding with his forked stick, lest he should fall into some pit. He grasped his tomahawk firmly, ready to defend himself if it became necessary, and finally came to where the narrow passage opened into a large apartment. It was totally dark. He paused, and listened; so profoundly still was it, that he could have heard the slightest breathing of a man or animal. Satisfied that there was no one within it, he determined to explore it fully, and to strike a light, that would reveal its character. With a steel and tinder that he carried to light his tobacco-pipe, he struck fire, and lighting a pine knot, with which he was provided, was enabled to take a survey of the cave.

There he saw benches, a rude table, beds, arms and ammunition; there was also food, liquor, and in short, everything that was wanted, to make whoever occupied the place, as comfortable as they could possibly be in such an abode. It was evident to the senses of Kua-ta-hù, that this subterranean abode, was not occupied by Indians, for there had evidently been too much labor exhausted upon it to meet the views of any of his race. It was supported by palisades, that, in his opinion, must have been rafted down the lake, as he had discovered no evidence of their having been cut near the spot. At the back part of the cave, was a small door, partly open. He passed through it, and found a narrow passage extending still farther,—a current of air almost extinguished his torch. Shielding it with the corner of his blanket, he kept on until the passage turned suddenly upward. The mystery of the holes in the lofty pine was solved; they had been cut there to let the confined air of the cave escape.

As it happened, the bandaleros had been out the night before, on one of their expeditions against a distant Whig family, and did not reach the lake until after daylight. They then deliberated as to whether it was good policy to embark and go to the cave at that time, as in all probability, Kua-ta-hu would be fishing, and discover them. They concluded to wait there until near night, as he usually left the lake and went home about three or four o'clock. They concealed themselves in a thicket, and the main part laid down to sleep, while the others stood as sentinels. Growing impatient, one of the men observed,

"There's no use of our skulking here, to avoid being seen by that cussed old Injun; the sooner we put him out of the way the better. It ought to have been done long ago. Now, I am for going to the cave, and if we find him skulking about the hill, or on the lake, in his canoe, I will bring my long rifle to bear on him."

"But suppose," said another, "that he should escape; then, in all probability, we should very soon have to change our quarters."

"Nothing ventured, nothing gained," returned the first speaker; "for my part, I want my breakfast, and if I have to shoot an Injun before I eat it, I shall relish it all the better. It is consummate, ridiculous folly, for us to be waiting here in this way: for my part, I apprehend more danger from being pursued by the neighbors of old Herron, the old Whig curmudgeon we robbed last night, than I do from this old Injun."

One after another of the gang fell in with this one's opinion, and they were soon after, paddling along towards Snake Hill.

Kua-ta-hu, after finishing his survey of the cave, was making his way out of the main passage, leading to the lake,—we say main passage, because Kua-ta-hu had discovered a very narrow passage, beside the one that he had entered, leading from the main room to the lake, in another direction; dug evidently for the purpose of retreating, if its inmates should happen at any time to be surprised in their subterraneous abode. While thus going out, he heard the sound of paddles. As he stood in the dark passage, he saw the thick evergreens open, and a large canoe filled with white men, disguised as Indians, glide into the passage.

There was no way for him to get out without taking the other passage; and fearing to take that, lest he should find others on the outer side, he went quietly back into the cave, and through the door that led into the tunnel that extended to the hollow tree. Having divined the use of the shaft, he felt tolerably secure where he was, and crouching along for some distance, quietly seated himself on the ground, determined to wait there until he could find an opportunity of escaping unseen, felicitating himself, at the same time, with the idea, that as he understood English very well, he should be able to ascertain who and what those men were, that had taken up their quarters in this strange, wild place.

"It is well," observed Sharpe, the man who had first broach ed the subject of starting for the cave, "for old Kua-ta-hu that he was not in sight, as I had determined to give him a dose of cold lead."

"I wish he had been," said Glanmore, "for somehow I have a presentiment that he will play the mischief with us yet."

"What will you give me for his scalp?" asked Sharpe.

"I will——why, I will give you one hundred and fifty dollars," answered Glanmore.

"Agreed," said Sharpe. "I will take my stand behind the log where you lay when you first discovered him, and while he is fishing, just opposite to it, in his accustomed place, I will convert him into fish-bait."

"Very well," said the chief. "Take your stand there to-morrow morning; but mind, now, you must bring his scalp, or you won't get the hundred."

"And fifty," continued the man, with a loud laugh.

"Ugh!" mentally exclaimed Kua-ta-hu, with an inward chuckle, as he overheard this conversation.

After the bandoleros had finished the meal, which it was their first care to provide, Sharpe, who had agreed to kill Kua-ta-hu, proposed to take his rifle and tomahawk, and go out to ascertain whether the old Indian's canoe might not be drawn up on the shore, as it was possible it might be, while he was in the woods. If he found it there, he would lie in ambush, and shoot him when he returned.

"Have to wait a great while," thought Kua-ta-hu, who con sidered himself fortunate in thus discovering that such dangerous inhabitants were in such close proximity to his favorite fishing and hunting grounds.

Sharpe returned in about an hour.

"Where's Kua-ta-hu's scalp?" said Glanmore.

"On him head," mentally exclaimed Kua-ta-hu.

"Oh! I didn't find any canoe," said Sharpe. "I went down the shore a long way. I think the lake has been too rough for fishing to-day. The wind has increased since we came in, and the swells are running very high."

"Good," mentally exclaimed Kua-ta-hu; "the waves drive Kua-ta-hu's canoe off;" and then he breathed easier, as he had been in great suspense lest the man might find his canoe and destroy it.

The bandits, as was their custom, now that they had got safely back to their quarters once more divided the spoils of the past night, and then made themselves merry over a bottle of brandy, that they had taken from the old Whig's cellar.

Growing communicative, as men generally do under the influence of good liquor, Sharpe ventured to address Glanmore as follows:

"I perceive," said he, "that something seems to hang heavily on your mind. Why, man, you look lately as though you had lost all your friends. Come, cheer up! Take another pull at Black Betty, and as the old Psalm says, tell us—

"'What it is that casts you down,
What it is that grieves you!'

And perhaps we can put matters all right. We are all your friends—we'll stick to you to the death. Come, out with it! You used to be the merriest fellow in the company, but since the affair of the soldier at your father's house, you are as solemn as an owl."

"My private feelings," returned Glanmore, haughtily, "are my own individual property, and no man must question me in regard to them."

"Bravely spoken, by G—!" said Sharpe. The blood mounted to Glanmore's forehead, as he sat moodily thinking of his affair of love. Sharpe, irritated by the reply of Glanmore, continued :—

"I shouldn't wonder if the chief had left a sweetheart somewhere, that he fears he may lose. I remember hearing him saying something about a Caroline somebody, in his sleep. Come, Glanmore, tell us who this Caroline is, and perhaps we may aid you in the matter."

Glanmore's face became still more flushed; and the rest of the band, mistaking his angry, burning countenance, for blushing bashfulness, set up a loud laugh, and cried out with one accord, "Come! come! Glanmore, you are caught! out with it, tell us who you are in love with, and what it is that clouds your brow."

Glanmore, finding that he was likely to be bored upon this matter, as he had not control enough over his men, who were principally much older than himself, and acknowledged no law except their own wills—to awe them into silence, concluded that he might as well tell them at once, why he was so altered in appearance and manner, at the same time, hoping that they might possibly aid him in consummating the final destruction of his rival, provided the plans he had already laid, did not succeed in accomplishing that object.

"If you will all swear," said Glanmore, "never to reveal

the secret, and to aid and assist me in the matter to the ut most of your power, I will let you into the mystery."

They all agreed to the proposition, and took the oath of eternal secrecy. After which, he made a full statement of his affair of love to them.

Kua-ta-hu drew near the door, and overheard every word that Glanmore spoke. After the recital was finished, he mentally exclaimed, "Glanmore no kill George Rushwood while Kua-ta-hu lives."

After some time, one of the band observed: "I would advise you to go to your father's to-night, and ascertain whether your cousin has succeeded in getting off to the army. It is possible too, that Rushwood may come home for a short time, as the American army are now lying only a few miles from your father's house. If he should happen to be at home, you might do the job for him yourself."

It was therefore agreed upon, that Glanmore should go home, and remain there concealed a few days; the operations of the band being in the mean time intrusted to the next in command.

Kua-ta-hu overheard them saying, "that they must go up the lake that night, to a point where they had concealed some provisions, and bring them down to the cave." Glanmore was to be carried in the canoe some distance up the lake, from whence he would strike out across the country for his father's place. At night they started on the proposed expedition. Kua-ta-hu was much rejoiced to hear that they were all going. They took the precaution to put out their lights. After they had been gone some minutes, Kua-ta-hu ventured from his hiding-place, and could just descry the canoe, as it glided away over the waves. He followed along the shore after the canoe, and perceiving them making for the shore, reached a tree, behind which he secreted himself very near the landing-place of Glanmore. After Glanmore landed, Kua-ta-hu followed him, dogging him as no one else could but an Indian.

When Glanmore reached his father's house, and all had become still there, Kua-ta-hu stole away quietly and went over to the house of Widow Rushwood. There was a light shining from the window. Kua-ta-hu peered cautiously in at the casement, and to his astonishment, saw George Rushwood and his mother in earnest conversation. He went quietly away, resolving to keep a strict watch upon Glanmore's movements, as he would now, probably, finding that George was at home, endeavor to take his life.

The next day, it was ascertained by the old Tory's family that Rushwood had arrived at home from the American camp.

When this intelligence came to the ears of Gordon Glanmore,

he exclaimed, mentally, "Now he is in my power. Ere to-morrow's sun shall ascend, the earth shall drink his blood. I will away to the cave, and summon some of my bravest and truest followers, and we will make a sure and certain end to the life of this hated rival of mine. But," continued he, "there may be danger in trusting these confederates of mine, too, for —no! I will not go to the cave, I,—yes, I will do the deed, he shall fall by my hand. Fool," muttered he, "fool that I am! I have gone too far already; I have trusted this love affair to the ears of those outlaws of mine, and who knows but that they may yet betray me."

Acting in accordance with this last resolve, he left the house as soon as it was dark, and armed with a pair of horse pistols, that were stuck into his girdle, stole across the fields, and entered a piece of woodland that approached very near the front of Widow Rushwood's house, and took a position there for the purpose of watching the movements of Lieut. Rushwood.

At length, the door opened and Rushwood came forth, and made his way directly towards Mansfield's house. Glanmore kept pace with him across the fields adjoining the road, not in the least suspecting that any human being was following him. But, as we before said, there was a human being not far behind him, who regarded every movement he made with extreme vigilance. That being, gentle reader, was Kua-ta-hu, who following him thus, and getting nearer and nearer to him, finally gave him the providential blow that saved the life of Lieut. Rushwood. When Kua-ta-hu struck him, it came so sudden and simultaneously with the terrific thunder-clap before described, that it led him to suppose, when he recovered from the stunning effects of the blow, that he had been slightly shocked by the electric fluid; yet he could hardly account by any mode of philosophical reasoning, for the wound upon his head. However much reason or philosophy failed to convince him of this, he was, nevertheless, well assured of one thing, and that was, that his rival had escaped unharmed, for he found, upon examining his pistol, that it was not discharged. The rain by this time was falling tremendously. Finding himself thus foiled in his dastardly attempt upon the life of his rival, he resolved to go back again to Rushwood's, having become convinced by the conversation, that Rushwood would not remain at Mansfield's that night, and that he would be off for the American camp on the morrow.

Kua-ta-hu, when he felled him to the earth, was on the point of striking him dead with his hatchet, but suddenly pausing, exclaimed, "No, me no kill him, ———kill him, that good." Meaning thereby, that according to the Indian method of revenge, it would be better for the injured party to have the satisfaction of killing the one who had injured him.

When he came to Rushwood's house, all was dark and silent within. He resolved to reach the cave and arouse his men. O! if he only had them with him how soon he would destroy his rival; but he dare not attack him single handed. He repaired to his father's stable, and mounting the fleetest horse it contained, rode furiously towards Saratoga lake. Kua-ta-hu followed, knowing pretty well where he was going, but he was distanced by the fleet horse, and turned back, for the purpose of informing Rushwood of his danger; but as he neared the house, he concluded, as it was a long way to the lake, Glanmore could not arrive there and bring men back with him before morning; so, wrapping himself in his blanket, he laid down in the woods, intending to warn Rushwood of his danger in the morning, but before he reached the house in the morning, George had left. He found that he had gone to the army, and would not return in a long time; and not thinking it prudent to frighten his mother by relating what he knew, he wisely held his peace, and returned to the south end of the lake, where he found his canoe.

Glanmore arrived at the cave, leaving his horse in the woods about two miles distant, aroused his sleeping men and related what had transpired. They immediately armed themselves, and set out with a full determination of burning Rushwood's house, and murdering him before morning. But before they reached it they found that it was so near morning, that they could not possibly accomplish their plan of destroying him before daylight; they therefore changed their purpose, and resolved to waylay and shoot him on the road. They made a wide circuit through the woodland on the back of the farms that lay along the highway. On coming to the spot before described, where George was shot at, they carefully examined the road, and finding that no horse had passed since the rain, considered themselves as sure now of their prey.

When George came in sight, they arranged themselves behind trees, and waited until he had just passed them, as they could then reveal themselves, and have a better chance to aim, but that fearful bound of the horse raised him and his rider above and out of the range of their fire. Perceiving themselves baffled, they sullenly made their way back to the cave.

Kua-ta-hu—deeming it unsafe to fish in the lake—after concealing his canoe in a different place from where he ordinarily did, went back to his wigwam, that was situated a little north of the present village of Saratoga Springs, and deliberated what he should do to prevent the fatal consequences that would ensue, if he did not apprise Rushwood of his danger but being the next day out in the woods, he was bitten in the leg by a rattlesnake. The remedies that the Indian race were in the habit of applying, for the cure of the bite of this venomous reptile, not being at hand, before he procured them his leg became fearfully swollen; he, however, at length found them, but the virus had infused itself so thoroughly throughout his system, that it was some days before he was able to again leave his wigwam, except to go three times each day to what is now known as the High Rock Springs, where he drank freely of the sparkling waters, that then flowed over the top of the conical rock through which they came forth. The lofty pine that afterwards fell across it, and caused the crack, through which the waters now escape near the ground, was then standing erect; and had Kua-ta-hu known that that tree was fated to destroy the beautiful fountain, that he believed to have been placed there by the Great Spirit, for the especial benefit of his red children, his hatchet would have soon hewed it down, and sent it crashing in another direction. He placed much reliance upon the medicinal qualities of this water, and believed that it was eminently useful in cleansing his system from the lurking effects of the rattlesnake's virus. During his confinement, which continued several days, he was in terrible anxiety lest the plans of the band, he had so providentially discovered, should be consummated, before he could inform their intended victim, so that he might frustrate them.

CHAPTER XII.

Plots and Plans.

When the bandits arrived at the cave, the chief was more despondent than ever. Twice had his rival been within his grasp, and twice had he escaped; once, as he almost believed, by the interposition of Providence; and again, as he believed, by an over-assurance on his part and that of his men.

It was night when they arrived at the cave, and but little was said by any one till after breakfast next morning, when one of the band remarked to Glanmore, "I don't see why you should wish to take the life of your rival; I have been thinking of a different plan, that might give you the entire control of the girl; then you might marry her if you pleased, and that would put an end to the matter; for after you had married her, forcibly or otherwise, George Rushwood would not wish of course, to make her his wife. He might then rave and rant as much as he pleased, but you may entirely avoid him; for as the British will probably be defeated soon, and our position here become untenable, you can take your money, that is buried here, and fly with the girl, where, by changing your name, you might never be recognized."

"What is your plan for getting possession of her," said the chief.

"It is this," continued he: "You know that the girl is at her father's house, now?"

"Yes, I have seen her there during the last two days."

"Well, as soon as it is dark to-night, we will march to old Mansfield's house. I have been itching for some time to handle the rusty dollars that he must have—for you know he is one of the richest men in these parts. We might as well make an end of him—as he will, if spared, raise the country, and pursue his daughter—and his wife, too. You see the policy of this?"

"Yes," responded the chief, moodily.

"Well, after this we will rob the house, and set fire to it: you in the mean time can secure the girl; and as the bodies will be consumed in the flames, people will take it for granted that she is consumed also—that will prevent pursuit."

"Well, what am I to do with the girl?" said the chief.

"Fly with her to my house in Schenectady. It is a retired place on the north side of the Mohawk. I will guide you there, and she can be kept there until you can make your future arrangements, as you wish."

"This all seems very well in theory," said the chief, but how will it work in practice? How can I ever look a wife in the face after being guilty of the death of her parents? And even had I the hardihood to do this, would she not detest and abhor me? Would she not fly from me the first opportunity that offered? I rather think I should have to keep her in a cage; and then she is such a courageous and high-spirited girl, that she would probably destroy herself; for at best, she loves me not."

"Secure her first, and the love will come afterwards," said the man.

"No, I think," returned the chief, "that I would rather throw myself into the lake, than to undertake such a job as that would be, if"——he paused a moment—"if I could first be assured that my rival was annihilated from the face of the earth."

"You are too sensitive in this matter," said the man; "are not your hands already deeply dyed in human blood? Are you not already an outlaw, and do you not know that if the Americans defeat the British, as it now seems probable they will, that you can never more be safe for a single moment in this county? In my opinion, if you are determined to have this girl, you had better strike now. If you delay this matter, probably in a few days Burgoyne will be defeated; the northern army will be partially disbanded, and that young ranger will return home; and then, if I am not mistaken in his metal, he will push this love affair to a successful issue. He will return fresh from a victorious battle-field; and, as the father of the girl is a thorough whig, he will take advantage of the auspicious moment; and then, if you and your band show your heads in that part, it is ten to one if he don't prove your ruin. I tell you, from what I saw in his eye, yesterday, he will be an ugly customer to deal with. If you should attack Mansfield's house, after he gets this fine young girl under his protection, you might as well attack a lion in his den."

"I feel the force of your argument," said the chief. A deep silence ensued. At length the chief arose, and paced the cave with hurried strides; seating himself again, he exclaimed—

"I have it now, your plan is good in part, but I think I can obviate some of the difficulties in the way. You know that every one in my neighborhood supposes me to be a prisoner in the British army. Now, if five or six of the band would go to Mansfield's house, and carry out your plan, I would take you," addressing the one who had concocted the plan, "and the balance of the band, and lie concealed at some little distance. I would procure a horse at my father's stable; and we would dress ourselves in common clothes. You secure the girl, and pretending to be Indians, be careful not to betray yourselves in this particular. Bring her with you as if to carry her away. After you pass the place where we are concealed, we will rush out, and come rapidly upon you. When we come up, you must pretend to resist; we will have a desperate sham fight. You must pretend to yield, after a while, and fly; I will wrest the girl from you, and assure her that having been a few days ago released from confinement, by being exchanged for British prisoners, I had arrived at home in the evening; that being aroused by perceiving the light of the burning house, I had flown to assist them, determined if the Tories or Indians had attacked the house, I would rescue her and her family, or perish in the attempt. I will leave one more in ambush, who must come running with apparently breathless haste, and say that a large body of Indians and Tories are advancing upon the neighborhood. I will then pretend to fly with her beyond the reach of danger, and we will make our way with her to your house. I think that in this way, I can conceal my real character, and inspire her with gratitude at least."

"Good!" exclaimed the whole gang, at once. "Capital plan! You will suceeed in winning the girl if you follow out your plan as well as you have commenced it."

"But the old man's money," said the chief, "you know I shall want a portion with my wife."

"For my part," said Sharpe, the man who claimed the honor of originating the plan, "I am willing that you should have all we get, for we have already more specie than we can readily dispose of in a long time, without exciting suspicion."

The band agreeing to this proposition, they made preparations for the expedition, and when darkness threw its sombre mantle over the bosom of the lake, they made their way towards Mansfield's residence.

CHAPTER XIII.

Attack upon Mansfield's house—Burning of the same—Supposed murder of Mr. Mansfield—Caroline a prisoner—Borne away by the Bandit Chief—Mrs. Sharpe.

THE thunder of the battle of Stillwater had that day been borne to the ears of Caroline Mansfield. Again and again, she went forth and listened to the tremendous roaring of volleys of musketry, and the awful thundering of the British artillery, that reverberated through the surrounding country. She would then go into the house, and throwing herself in the attitude of prayerful supplication, earnestly implore the Almighty Ruler of the Universe to spare unscathed, if it seemed to him meet, the brave youth of her heart; who was then no doubt mingling in the terrible conflict that came home to her ears on the wings of the wind.

Old Widow Rushwood also heard the distant roar of the battle; she too prayed with that deep and earnest agony, that none but a loving mother could manifest, for the safety of her son. But she had no one to comfort her, she was alone: none to breathe a word of consolation; none to pour oil upon the troubled waters of her soul.

At length the distant roar died away; fainter and fainter it came, and then as the twilight came there was a deep calm, rendered awful by the contemplation that probably now hundreds of brave men that had that day gone forth to battle, were lying now all weltering in gore, and locked in the cold, icy embrace of death.

Caroline Mansfield felt the terrible effect of this calm, and after repeatedly listening to discover whether the engagement was renewed, offered up a prayer for the safety of her country, and her lover, if he were not already slain. She then retired, and overcome by the fearful excitement of the day, she sunk into a nervous slumber, and dreamed that her lover had been slain in the battle; that she had gone forth to gaze once more upon his features; that she was passing over and among the heaps of dead soldiers and officers that were scattered over the battle-field, and that as she discovered the pale corpse of ner lover, a band of painted and plumed savages came suddenly upon her; she uttered a scream that awoke her. She heard some one knocking at the door. She stole softly into her father's chamber and informed him of it. Her heart beat high with hope, it might be George, who had returned to bring the tidings of the battle.

Mr. Mansfield was a cautious as well as a courageous man, and as calls at that hour of the night were rather suspicious, after lighting a candle, he took an old sword from its hanging place in the bed-room, and advancing to the window, inquired who was there. The fellow, thinking of the caution that had been given the band, not to betray themselves by using their native language, answered Kua-ta-hu, trying to give the name as deep a guttural sound as possible. The artifice succeeded. Mr. Mansfield, thinking that Kua-ta-hu had come to warn him of some approaching danger, opened the door without further delay; but in an instant several Indian figures sprang towards him. He endeavored to defend himself, and did successfully, for a time; but at length he received a blow on the head, from a tomahawk that was thrown at him, and fell apparently dead upon the floor. The assailants then pursued the affrighted Caroline, who was vainly endeavoring to fly with her mother. The old lady seeing the savages, as she supposed them to be, coming through the hall, from whence she and Caroline were endeavoring to escape by a back door, swooned and fell, and Caroline was instantly seized, and though she struggled resolutely, was held firmly by the superior strength of three men, while the rest ransacked the house. Finding it useless to struggle, she assumed a statue-like calmness, and gazed fearfully at the bodies of her father and mother, that lay on the floor, apparently dead.

The robbers at length finished their search, and brought forth several hundred silver dollars,—time was precious to them, as they were in the midst of an extensive settlement. They felt of the bodies: the old lady appeared entirely lifeless, and the blood flowed plentifully from the wounded father; he did not appear to be quite dead, but they nevertheless supposed that he had received a mortal wound. They drew the bodies into the bed-room, and fastened the door firmly. One of the gang, whispering in a very low tone to another, remarked, "If they are not dead, the fire will finish them." They then set fire to the house in several places, taking care to pile a heap of combustibles against the door of the bed-room, where the bodies lay, and set fire to it.

While these fearful preparations were going forward, the dauntless Caroline stood pale as marble, firmly grasped by two men; but when she saw the flames that were to devour her parents, begin to rise and lap the partition against which they lay; and when the robbers seized her, and rudely bore her out of her father's house, ah! then the world was a blank to her. She fell into a dreadful swoon, from which she did not awake until she found herself surrounded by four men, who were applying water to her face to arouse her. They hurried away with the inanimate form of Caroline, and after passing the point where the chief lay concealed, saw him come rushing on towards them; his demeanor was furious and determined, but they spoke to him and assured him, "that there was no necessity for the proposed sham-fight and rescue, as the girl was senseless, and unless means were immediately taken to restore her, she would probably never breathe again."

Deeply disappointed in being thus frustrated in this important manœuvre, he took the apparently lifeless form of Caroline on the horse before him, and soon arrived at a small brook, where he restored her to consciousness. Perceiving herself to be surrounded by Americans, she uttered a wild exclamation, and recognizing Glanmore, as he bent over her, upbraided him with having been the cause of her capture.

"Believe me, Miss Mansfield," said Glanmore; "when I tell you that you are entirely mistaken. I was but a few days ago released from confinement within the British lines. I arrived at home this very night. I saw the flames of your father's house, and determined to save you and your family, as I suspected they had been attacked by Indians or Tories. I aroused these friends of mine, who were at my father's house, and flew to the scene of destruction. I found that the house had apparently been robbed, as I found no one about. I rushed in to see if any one could be found, but as I opened the door, the flames burst out, and it was impossible to enter. By the light of the burning house, I discovered bloody tracks leading in this direction—I hurried on the road as the tracks led me—I overtook five Indians carrying you away. After a desperate struggle I succeeded in wresting you from them. Two or three of them were wounded when they fled. I brought you hither, as this was the nearest water that I could reach, to restore you to consciousness.—"

At this moment, one of the band came running with breathless haste, and informed them that a large party of Tories and Indians had attacked the neighborhood, and that he had barely escaped from their rapid movements.

"We must fly," said the chief, "for after sacking our neighborhood, they will probably sweep on further, O! my poor father and mother!" ejaculated he, apparently in a paroxysm of agony, "I would fain defend you, but alas! there is no use of five men's attempting to face hundreds. Caroline," said he, "I will defend you; I will carry you out of the reach of these merciless savages. Fly with me! time is precious!"

"No, let me go back and die upon the funeral pile of my parents," said she. "If you carry me away, it will be against my will. O! release me, and let me return and throw myself into the flames of my father's house!"

Finding that she was not to be persuaded, he exclaimed, "It is folly, it is madness, Miss Mansfield, to talk thus! When the excitement of this terrible night is over, you will thank me for preserving your life." So saying, he, by the assistance of his men, lifted the form of the trembling girl to his saddle.

"I cannot, I will not go!" she exclaimed, "I cannot go forward to meet a worse death than that I have escaped."

"Be calm, Miss Mansfield," said Glanmore, "I will protect you, as far as I can from all harm; these friends of mine will aid me in so doing. You cannot suppose that the friend of your youth means to leave you. No, Caroline, I will not suffer you to remain here to be slaughtered, or carried away a captive by the savages."

Finding that it was in vain to expostulate, Caroline became calm, and with a resolve that she would escape the first opportunity, was carried forward by the ruffianly bandoleros.

They treated her with great tenderness, but vainly did Glanmore endeavor to assure her that he had rescued her. No, she had overheard the whisper at her father's house in relation to the disposal of her parents' bodies. It convinced her that those men were not Indians, and she believed that all Glanmore had told her was a base fabrication to deceive her. She believed him to have been one of the number, and she was now confirmed in her former suspicions relative to his being a Tory. The deep sorrow that she felt for the loss of her parent, was too deep, too full, to allow her to weep, and so with dreadful calmness she submitted to her fate.

All night, and all next day, did they travel with her, and not until late the next night did they reach the place of their destination. It was a rude log-house, near the Mohawk River. They halted a few rods from it, and one of the men, addressing Caroline, said: "Here is my house—here you will be beyond the reach of danger—and here you are welcome to stay until your friend can ascertain when it will be safe for you to return." He then went forward to arouse his family, "as he did not wish," as he said, "to frighten them by appearing before the house with so large a company." His wife, he said, "was a nervous woman, and might go off into one of her spells." At length a light gleamed from the house, and the party advanced and were ushered in. The woman of the house met Caroline in a graceful and lady-like manner, that greatly astonished her, being so different from the usual address of the wives of back-woodsmen. She expressed herself as deeply sympathizing with her in her misfortunes. She was certain she must be greatly fatigued by so long a journey, performed under such uncomfortable circumstances, and hurrying about, prepared a very comfortable supper, of which she urged Caroline to partake. Caroline sat down at the table, but she could swallow nothing. No, her grief was too deep and poignant to allow her to eat. After which, the woman escorted her to a neat room, in which was a comfortable bed, and corresponding furniture. "This, my dear young lady," said she, "will be your room while you stay with us; so make yourself comfortable, and may God enable you to bear up under your bitter trials." Bidding her a kind "Good-night," she left Caroline, and in a moment returned, saying, "I forgot to give you the key of your room," at the same time handing it to her. "I shall be obliged to lodge these strangers in the large room through which you passed, and I thought you might wish to lock your door." After she was gone, Caroline offered up a prayer to her heavenly Father, that he would support her in this trying hour; after which she locked her door, and retired for the night. The great fatigue she had endured so completely overcame her that she fell into a profound sleep, from which she did not awake until the next morning. Mrs. Sharpe took good care to lock the door of the large room adjoining Caroline's, as she had been warned against leaving any outlet through which she might escape; and as her husband and the balance of the party were in a distant part of the house, they talked freely of the success of their plans thus far. Mrs. Sharpe complimented the bandit chief on the beauty of his fair captive; but Sharpe was of the opinion that it would take him a long time to win her heart by gentle means, if he succeeded no better than he had since he had got her into his power. The deep and deceitful Mrs. Sharpe, who was withal of a romantic turn of mind, eagerly listened to a recital of all the plans and operations thus far, and delighted with the novelty of the thing, freely gave her advice for furthering them, promising to use every artifice in her power to bring matters to a successful issue.

"As the young gentleman does not seem inclined," said she, "to resort to any violent means to win his lady, now that she is in his power, whenever he thinks fit to use it, I would advise him, for some time at least, to treat her with no more than common politeness. This will lull her suspicions, and lead her to suppose that he has really taken a disinterested part in the matter; and the more effectually to lull her suspicions, I would advise him to let me write a few love-letters, purporting to come from some young lady at a distance. He can place them in his coat pocket, and leaving it in the house, go out to-morrow for some alleged purpose, and while he is out, I will take up the coat, and as it will exhibit nothing more than female curiosity, I will probe the pocket and take out the letters and read them in her presence, pretending to have discovered a great secret. There must be one, also, that must be written in your own hand, and dated recently. It must be wrapped up carefully, addressed to the lady, but not sealed, as though you had not sent it. It must reply to the last letter of your imaginary lady-love, and must contain a proposition of marriage."

This was considered a good plan, and Mrs. Sharpe sat down and wrote three short, but sweet, letters, and then directed Glanmore how to write one in reply to her last. They purported to come from a young lady at a distanee, and it appeared from the answer that they had accumulated at his house while he had been a prisoner in New York. "After your return," said she, with a knowing wink, "from the expedition you propose to take in order to ascertain whether it will be safe for Miss Mansfield to return, I will furnish you with another letter, in which you shall be informed of the death of your lady, and then you must begin to woo Miss Mansfield as a balm for a broken heart." After concocting this very deeply romantic plan, as she considered it, she retired, consoling herself with the contemplation of her wonderful ingenuity.

It was late in the morning before any of the inmates of the house arose, except the man who noiselessly guarded Caroline's room. Mrs. Sharpe went to Miss Mansfield's room, and roused her, fearing, as she said, "that she would sleep too much—it was not proper to sleep too long at a time, after being greatly exhausted with fatigue. The sleep then was too heavy, and had a tendency to injure one. She would advise her, by all means, to rise and take some coffee; it would invigorate her so much, and then she might, if she chose, lie down, and refresh herself with sleep during the day."

Caroline heard all this artful woman's fair speeches with distrust. She assured her "that she felt extremely ill, and although she might sit up for a brief time, and take some refreshment, yet she would be extremely happy if Mrs. Sharpe would send them in to her room, and at the same time would bring her a bible, as she was in the habit of reading a portion of Scripture each morning before breakfast."

A large family bible was brought in, and laid upon a small

table, and also the coffee, and some cakes, and sundry other delicacies. Mrs. Sharpe "did not wish to intrude, but if Miss Mansfield would read a portion of Scripture aloud, she would be pleased to listen to it. It was not common for her to have the pleasure of having pious and educated young ladies at her house, since Mr. Sharpe had moved from the city into the backwoods."

Caroline complied; but Mrs. Sharpe was not prepared for what followed. After Caroline had finished reading, she knelt down and prayed. However, the hypocritical woman must carry out her hypocrisy in order to be consistent; and so, after Miss Mansfield had ceased praying, she made a very appropriate prayer in behalf of the orphan who had been thrown by the necessities of life, as she expressed it, under her especial care. Thus hypocrisy ever overleaps itself, for Caroline Mansfield saw at a glance that this cold and formal prayer did not come from the deep fountains of the soul; and further, that in requesting her to read, and tarrying while she prayed, she had transgressed the rules of etiquette, as no real lady would presume to ask such a privilege of one in her circumstances.

After Mrs. Sharpe had left, she partook of some slight refreshment, and turning to the Word of Life for consolation, she was particularly struck with the beautiful feminine delicacy of the hand, in which the records of the family were therein registered. She noticed it the more particularly, as the hand was uncommonly beautiful. Mrs. Sharpe came in to remove the breakfast, and Caroline was at that moment looking at the family record. Thinking that she would smother in some degree the feelings of abhorrence she had conceived for this woman, she observed,—

"This is an uncommonly beautiful hand, Mrs. Sharpe."

"Yes," returned Mrs. Sharpe, "I always keep the family record myself. My husband writes a hurried business hand, and he always would insist that I should make the entries instead of him."

One of the band from the cave arrived soon after breakfast, and informed the chief "that old Mansfield had somehow or other escaped from the burning house. He had come into the possession of the knowledge in this way: After those of the band who were left behind by him when he came away with the captive girl, had got back to the cave, they were extremely uneasy lest the attack upon Mansfield's house would arouse the people in that thickly settled neighborhood, and bring them out to search for the perpetrators of the deed, and that they would be found in the cave, and destroyed. They therefore sent him, the next night, to reconnoitre the place, and see what he could do about matters there. He arrived in the vicinity during the night, and saw that the house was entirely consumed. As he came along in sight of Widow Rushwood's house, he saw a light burning there. He cautiously approached the window from whence it issued, and peering in, saw a number of armed men; then he descried Mr. Mansfield lying upon the bed, with his head bandaged; old Mrs. Mansfield was sitting by the bed-side, apparently well, as she was administering medicine to the husband. The men were talking about the attack upon the house, and seeming to hunt out the perpetrators of the act. He hurried back to the cave, and the men then desired that he should come to him and urge him to come back to the cave immediately, as they thought now they had better disband, and each one take his share of the spoils and go his way. One of the men had learned that the Americans had defeated Burgoyne in an action fought the day the robbery was committed, and they now considered their position insecure in that part of the country. They had made up their minds that if he did not come back to the cave in three days, they would take the money and divide it, and then abandon the cave."

Upon the receipt of this intelligence, Glanmore hastily prepared to depart; and after cautioning Mrs. Sharpe in no event to let Caroline escape from the house, took his departure, with his men, for the cave.

In the confusion of the moment, Mrs. Sharpe forgot about the letters; but recollecting about them as soon as the men had left the house, and not wishing to be baffled in carrying out her plan, she called the chief, and when he turned back she exclaimed,—"I forgot to tell you to leave the letters with me. I will manage them—just leave them with me, if you please. I will make good use of them in your behalf." Not caring much about them, he objected at first, but perceiving that Mrs. Sharpe would distrust his confidence in her, as she plainly exhibited it in her countenance, he thought proper to yield to her solicitations.

After he was gone, she was nettled with the idea of putting her plan with regard to the letters into operation. During the forenoon she went and knocked lightly at Caroline's door. Caroline arose from her bed, where she was vainly endeavoring to soothe her troubled spirit with sleep, unlocked the door, which she kept locked, fearing lest Glanmore might invade the sanctity of her chamber, and let Mrs. Sharpe in.

"I have finished my morning duties," said she, "and concluded that I would come in and try to comfort you. I have some news to tell you that may contribute towards that result. Your friend has started on his way back to your home, to ascertain whether it will be safe for you to return. If he finds it to be so, he will return, with some of his neighbors, and a comfortable conveyance, and take you back as soon as possible But, by-the-bye, as I went into the room where he slept, I discovered this package where he had dropped it. He was gone; so I took it up. I wished to ascertain if it was valuable, so that I might take care of it accordingly; but upon opening it, I found that it was a package of love-letters that he had received from some young lady, and I declare there was another, written by himself, in answer to the lady's last letter, in which he makes a formal proposal of marriage to her. Now you know that ladies, impelled by the natural curiosity of the sex, always take the privilege of reading one's love-letters, when they accidentally fall into their hands, and if you are willing, I would like to read them to you.

Caroline, divining that these letters had something to do with her own case, expressed a desire to hear them. Mrs. Sharpe went on to read the letters; but as Caroline glanced at the address, she at once saw they were in the same beautiful handwriting that she had discovered in the family bible. The truth flashed on her mind in an instant. She saw now through the character of Mrs. Sharpe; she was deeply engaged in the plot for her destruction, and she resolved to fly from the house the first opportunity, preferring, as she did, anything rather than being the prey of a man who would thus deeply imbrue his hands in human blood.

Acting under this resolve, she feigned to throw off the deep load of sorrow that weighed her down, and exhibited such a degree of cheerfulness, that Mrs. Sharpe really believed her plan would have the effect she wished.

Caroline wished to gain a knowledge of the locality of the house, and to this end, she requested Mrs. Sharpe to walk out with her, as she thought it would be beneficial to her to take the fresh air. She perceived that the house was on the Mohawk river, and learned from Mrs. Sharpe, that it was the only house in that section. Their nearest neighbor was four miles off, and to reach them one must travel through a dense forest. Mr. Sharpe had chosen this location on account of the excellent quality of the land, as he doubted not when his countrymen should defeat, and drive away the invaders, the place would be speedily settled.

That afternoon Caroline prepared herself, and succeeding in opening the window of her room, she got out of it, and fled across a small field that lay adjoining the house, intending to follow down the bank of the Mohawk until she reached the house of some settler, who would guide her on to Albany;

where she had friends living. Mrs. Sharpe did not however let a half-hour escape without visiting Caroline's room, when she listened at the key-hole, or made some excuse for entering; but coming now to the room, she heard no noise; she peered through the key-hole, she could discover no one; she knocked lightly at the door, but received no answer; she knocked loudly, and still receiving no answer, she made an attempt to force the door; failing in this, she ran out of the house to summon her two sons, who were working in a field at some distance. As she crossed the little inclosure through which Caroline had passed, she saw the imprint of a delicate female foot in the light alluvial soil: she followed on the track, but losing it, she summoned her sons, and an Indian, that was helping the work that day. The sagacious Indian took the track of Miss Mansfield, and followed by the two boys and Mrs. Sharpe, traced the track to a swamp, where they saw Caroline trying to make her way over the bogs and old logs that lay scattered about. Perceiving her pursuers, Caroline felt that she was discovered, and the sudden revulsion of feeling caused her to swoon. She was conveyed back to the house by the Indian, and then Mrs. Sharpe speedily applied restoratives that brought her back to consciousness. As soon as Mrs. Sharp saw she was recovered, she exclaimed, "My dear young friend, I fear that the troubles through which you have passed, have so far operated upon you as to cause your mind to wander from its usual course. We found you just now in a swamp, nearly a mile from the house. I shall, in order to prevent you again wandering away, be obliged to leave you in this room, where there are no windows, for a day or two, and keep the key myself, as it is impossible that I can keep an eye on you the whole time. I will furnish you with a light, and everything comfortable, and I trust that in a day or two you will get over these aberrations of mind."

Caroline saw that she was to be now made a prisoner, but still was willing that Mrs. Sharpe should think that an alienated mind had caused her to escape, if she was really sincere in what she said. "I don't know," said she, "but my mind does wander, for my head aches terribly."

"It is very natural to suppose that it does," said Mrs. Sharpe, "considering what you have passed through. You had better try now to compose yourself to rest, but first take a little of this tincture, it is sedative in its operation, and will quiet your nerves."

Caroline took the mixture and smelled of it as she put it to her mouth, and pretended to sip it, and found that it was deeply drugged with opium. "I will take a little more of it, bye and bye," said she.

Mrs. Sharpe now informed her that she must go out and get tea. "Well," said she, "I must keep the key of your door, for it is a great providence that we found you so soon, as you would probably have sunk in that swamp you were in."

As soon as Caroline was left alone, she mentally exclaimed, "Then I am indeed a captive and a prisoner, and this artful and hypocritical woman is my jailor, and thinks to drug me with opium to keep me quiet, but in this she shall be mistaken." And thus saying, she pushed the glass containing the drug from her, and sinking back in her chair, tears for the first time came to her relief. It was the first time she had wept since her appalling calamity, but at length she became calm, and with heroic fortitude resolved that before she would submit to the dreadful fate that seemed to await her, she would perish in defending herself.

CHAPTER XIV.

Kua-ta-hu determines to warn Lieut. Rushwood of his danger —Visits the ruins of Mansfield's house—Is suspected by some of the neighbors—Goes to the cave at Snake Hill—Gets a clue to the whereabouts of Miss Mansfield—Rescues her from her keeper—Comes near being discovered by the bandits—Arrives at the High Rock Spring—Urges her to drink, alleging that the water was a " Great Medicine."

When Kua-ta-hu recovered so as to go out, he resolved at once to make his way to the American camp, and inform Lieut. Rushwood of his danger. As the residence of his mother lay nearly in his course, he determined to call there and see her, so that he could inform George of her condition, whatever it might be. He called at Mrs. Rushwood's house the day after Mr. Mansfield's house was burned. He was surprised to find a large number of men there, and listened eagerly to the recital of the circumstances. Some of the men who had heard Mr. Mansfield say, " that when he asked who was there, he was answered Kua-ta-hu," were strong in the belief that he was the one who led the party of Indians there. They brought Kua ta-hu, therefore, to Mr. Mansfield's bedside, and asked Mansfield whether he supposed he was one of the gang. Mr. Mansfield assured them that there was no one in the party that looked at all like him; and farther, that he should want the strongest kind of proof before he could believe Kua-ta-hu to be guilty of doing one an injury, whom he supposed had been instrumental in saving his life; it was not in accordance with the general character of the Indian. He did not believe that Kua-ta-hu was any way implicated in the transaction; no, rather than think that Kua-ta-hu was guilty, he would sooner suspect that some of his Tory countrymen had disguised themselves as Indians, and committed the outrage upon him. Kua-ta-hu was highly pleased with Mansfield's good opinion of him.

Mr. Mansfield then gave Kua-ta-hu an account of the transaction, and informed him that he believed the party had carried off his daughter. "It was at first supposed," said he, "that her remains would be found among the ashes of the house, but they have been thoroughly raked, and no traces of human remains have been found. Diligent search has been made," said he, "by my neighbors, but no traces of her can be found."

The truth flashed upon Kua-ta-hu's mind—the party that attacked them must have been the band of Glanmore, and in all probability Caroline Mansfield was now a prisoner in the cave. His first impulse was to inform Mr. Mansfield and his friends, who had just come in from an expedition in search of Caroline, of what he knew and suspected; but then they might have carried her elsewhere. In that event, attacking the cave would effect nothing except the capture of the gang, for it was probable that wherever she was, she was securely guarded.

Mr. Mansfield requested him to go in search of his daughter, promising to reward him. Kua-ta-hu spoke not a word in reply, but with that apparently stoical indifference, characterizing his race, strode away, revolving in his mind, whether he should go in pursuit of the young lady, or to inform her lover of his danger, as he had resolved. However, George Rushwood was a "brave," and as he could probably take care of himself better than the "white squaw," he would go in search of her, and so he bent his way towards the cave.

It was now nearly night, and by the time he arrived at the hill, it was quite late. He looked out upon the lake and saw a canoe gliding away from the cave. He could discern that there were but four men in it, the balance of the gang must be in the cave. He placed his ear against the ventilating pine, and heard the sound of voices. He stood there and listened for a long time, but could hear nothing distinctly. At length he saw four or five men come scrambling up out of the mouth of the cave. As they came up the hill, they halted just below the foot of the pine, where Kua-ta-hu stood.

"It seems first rate," said one of them, "to get out of that old hole and get a snuff of fresh air."

"Yes," said another, "but I suppose if the chief knew that we had come up here, he would be frightened out of his wits, for fear of our tracks being discovered by old Kua-ta-hu. I guess he don't come over here around the lake now, but if he should, I don't believe he could discover our tracks all among this dry pine foliage."

"I hope," said another, "that he will succeed in securing his girl, now that he has got in possession, or rather in reversion, as old dad's parchment reads"

"Yes," returned another, "but if that gal don't give him the slip before he gets back to Sharpe's I will give you my head for a foot-ball."

"No, I think Mrs. Sharpe is so deeply interested in the affair," said another, "that she will stick to her like wax. She prides herself upon her management of such affairs, and rather than fail in this attempt, she will spend all her time for a month. You know I was there when we carried her off, and if I am any judge in the matter, it will be some time before she gets away from her."

"Well, let's see," said another; "how long before the chief will be back? He has probably got across the lake by this time. It must take him at least four days to go there and back, and then we are to make one more attempt on old Mansfield's life, and then we will be clear from this spot. For my part, I am getting tired of this. I want now to get off with my part of the shiners, where I can take the good of them."

"You musn't be in too much of a hurry," said another; "you know the chief has got to be married, and that is no small job, especially when you must wed your bride by force of arms! And then, poor fellow, he must have a short honey-moon; you don't mean to take him from the arms of his loving wife, right away, do you?" continued the man with a sneer.

"O, no," said another; "let him enjoy it if he can, but then he must not expect to keep us all waiting here for him too long, whilst he is fondling his loving bride." And then a low suppressed laugh ran through the company.

Kua-ta-hu had heard enough for his purpose; and as the bandoleros were busily talking among themselves in an undertone, he stole quietly away. He must now follow Glanmore; he must prevent the marriage; he knew now where Caroline was; he had been to Sharpe's house. Yes! it was on the bank of the Mohawk, and was a long way off; if he was speedy he could get there before the chief and his men got there; and so without more ado he started on an Indian short path, and reached the Mohawk before morning. Pursuing his way up the river he found an Indian canoe, that had been swept down the river, lying upon its bank. He launched it, and made his way up the river in it for some miles. He then moored it, and by daylight was near the residence of Sharpe, where Caroline was confined. Keeping a sharp look-out from the woods in the rear of the house, into which Caroline had before escaped, he saw the two youths go off to their work. He kept quiet, and at length he saw two women come out of the house, and make directly towards him, across the small enclosure. He was secreted behind a large chesnut. As they approached him he saw that the younger of the two was Caroline Mansfield. Her eyes were red and swollen, and her cheek was pale as marble. Kua-ta-hu heaved a deep sigh, as he saw this lovely flower thus faded and withering beneath the terrible blast that had swept over her. As they neared him he heard Mrs. Sharpe observe to her:—

"We will get over here and pick up some of these chestnuts, this little employment will have a good influence upon your spirits."

They approached very near him—they were gathering chestnuts under the very tree behind which he stood, his eyes gleamed with revenge, as the woman who was placed as a guard over his former benefactress opposed him—she came very near—he wriggled like a cat just ready to pounce upon her prey, and as she turned her back towards the tree, he sprang towards her with the agility of a tiger, and with one blow of his tomahawk, laid her senseless upon the ground.

Caroline was terrified when she saw a huge savage spring from the tree, but in an instant she recognized the form and features of Kua-ta-hu. In one instant the savage assured her by a smile, and a sign of silence, that he had come to rescue her. She felt assured now that the hour of her deliverance was at hand. She confided in the sterling principles of this savage, rude and hideous as he was. Instantly he made a sign for her to follow him, and hurrying through the wood, he looked back and saw that the pale and weak Caroline was giving out. He caught her up in his arms, and trotted away with her as if she had been but an infant. He reached his canoe, and placed her therein, and aided by the current, shot rapidly down the Mohawk. Long before sunset he arrived at the point where they must debark. He lay there in ambush until night, fearing that if he struck up across the country, he might encounter the party who were making their way from the cave to the place where he had been. He set out with his charge as soon as it was dark, after having endeavored to strengthen her by giving her some pounded parched corn. They kept on until daylight. Soon after daylight, he heard the approach of footsteps. In an instant he laid his ear to the ground, and distinguished the heavy tread of several men. Casting a hurried glance around, he saw a large tree with a hollow trunk, and an aperture large enough to admit a person to enter. He thrust Caroline into the aperture, and although a huge black snake lay coiled on one side of the hollow, yet she stood there heroically, and moved not, nor uttered a sound, while Kua-ta-hu stood behind the tree and watched the approaching party. Suddenly, as they neared him, and were pursuing a course that would bring them some rods away from the tree, a huge black snake started away from before them, and raising his head high from the ground, glided directly towards the tree wherein his mate lay. One of the party, attracted by the unusually large size of the snake, bounded away after it.

"Stop," cried the foremost of the band, who was no other than the bandit chief. The man halted. "You had better let that snake go, and save your strength for other purposes, as you will be tired enough by the time you get where we are going."

Kua-ta-hu supposed when he saw the snake coming, that he was the mate of the one that he had discovered laying in the hollow tree—if the man kept on he would discover him. However, he stood with that firmness, that characterizes the Indian in ambush, and to his great joy, saw the man obey the admonitions of his chief.

Caroline saw the huge monster come with lightning rapidity into the tree, but she had recognized the voice of Glanmore, and that was more terrible to her than the lion's roar, or the panther's cry, and so she stood with heroic fortitude and watched the hissing reptiles, that raised their necks and seemed ready to spring upon her.

Kua-ta-hu saw the party move along, and almost resolved to send a rifle ball through the head of their leader, but reflecting that "prudence was the better part of valor," he wisely kept still until they disappeared over a small hill.

Turning to Caroline with extreme satisfaction, after seeing the two writhing monsters that had been confronting her in the hollow tree, he exclaimed, "brave squaw," and then they made their way onward. He now felt relieved, in a great measure, from apprehension. He was assured that he must somewhere cross the trail of the party, and now that he had, and had seen them so that there could be no mistake, he went joyfully along; but soon he saw that he was to meet with new troubles: the sky was overcast and the rain began to fall; true, this would obliterate the trail he had made, and hinder any one from tracking him, but then he feared that Caroline would be unable to proceed, and would moreover fall sick from the effects of such exposure and fatigue; however, to guard against such an event, he wrapped her in his own blanket, and when she could no longer travel, he took her up in his stalwart arms and doggedly pursued his way.

Caroline, although suffering from fatigue, want of sleep, and exposure to the pelting storm, that now came driving furiously upon them, felt comparatively happy. She was now free from her persecutors, and she felt assured that Kua-ta-hu was carrying her towards her friends, yes, she felt more secure in the wild forest, with this savage, than she did with those of her own race, that she had escaped from, whom she considered as far beneath savages.

All that night did Kua-ta-hu carry his precious burden, who had fallen asleep in his arms, overcome and exhausted as she was by fatigue. Kua-ta-hu sat down occasionally to rest himself, during the night. He had at first resolved to carry the girl directly to her father's, but the driving storm induced him to seek the nearest shelter. As his wigwam was many miles nearer the Widow Rushwood's, he altered his course during the night, and by daylight came very near his wigwam. Caroline awoke, and being greatly refreshed, was able to proceed. They at length came to the spot where the present village of Saratoga is located. He could not pass by his favorite spring without taking a draught of the bright and sparkling water that came gurgling from the top of the rock. He took a refreshing drink and then urged Miss Mansfield to partake of it with him ;-assuring her that it was good for her, and a "great medicine."

They who now visit this delightful spot, can have but a slight conception of the place at that time, covered as it was, with a dense, dark forest, with a dark savage standing by the High Rock Spring, and urging a white maiden to partake of its sparkling waters, that are now quaffed with avidity by the thousands that visit it annually. Caroline partook of it slightly, from the cup of her Indian preserver, and then they made their way to the wigwam of Kua-ta-hu.

The drizzling Autumnal rain continued for two days; during this time, Caroline greatly revived, both in strength and spirits. The smoked bass that Kua-ta-hu broiled for her, and the cakes he made her from his pounded corn, was substantial food, and Caroline partook of them freely, not omitting to drink heartily each day, of the sparkling waters that he brought her from the High Rock Spring. Each night he carefully closed his wigwam, when he made up a comfortable bed for his fair guest, composed of skins and dried grass; and sheltering himself outside the wigwam, stood sentinel until daylight, to repel any attack that might be made upon him by Caroline's persecutors, if they should happen to discover him; but there was no necessity for this precaution, he was not molested.

Caroline, after they arrived at the wigwam, entreated him to tell her if he knew aught of her parents. He remained silent for some time. Caroline supposed from this that he knew the fate of her parents, and wished to conceal it from her to avoid wounding her feelings. At length, when he had smoked his pipe, he informed her of all he had discovered of the cave, and of his subsequent visit to the neighborhood, and that her mother was well, and her father likely to recover from his wound. Caroline was overjoyed, a mountain was instantly removed from her heart; and she urged Kua-ta-hu to guide her home at once. The prudent and cautious Indian, however, assured her that it was imprudent to go until the storm was over. Finally, the clouds dispersed, and the sun came out. Caroline went forth from the wigwam; and never did the sun shine so brightly in her imagination before. The noise of the drops that fell from the dripping trees, the chatting of the squirrels that leaped from branch to branch—all seemed like music in her ears; and the rain-drops that hung upon the ends of the foliage of the lofty pines, appeared like diamonds placed there to brighten the cheerful scene.

Kua-ta-hu now made preparations for starting with his charge. He produced an Indian dress and blanket that had belonged to a son of his, that had died some two years before, and desired her to put them on. She laughed at the idea of decking herself out in feathers and paint, but Kua-ta-hu assured her that he considered it necessary. If he should encounter any of the Snake-hill bandits in his journey, they would recognize her, and recapture her; and if any other white men came across him they would certainly inquire of him what he was doing with a white girl travelling through the forest. That would delay them; and if the whites should happen to be tories, they might lead to other unpleasant consequences.

Caroline perceiving that Kua-ta-hu had good objects in view, complied with his request; and after he showed her the use of all the different articles, he left the wigwam, and she proceeded to dress herself in Indian costume. After dressing herself, Kua-ta-hu came in, and proceeded to paint her in the most approved style, with various colors; her dark eyes and long raven hair, that was now combed down on her shoulders, personified a gay Indian admirably. Kua-ta-hu expressed himself pleased with her appearance; he then set out on his journey, after going to the rock spring and taking a hearty drink, with his disguised charge, of the sparkling and favorite beverage.

CHAPTER XV.

Glanmore arrives at Sharpe's—Finds Mrs. Sharpe senseless—Is informed by an Indian that Kua-ta-hu has been seen on the Mohawk—Returns to the cave, after vainly endeavoring to overtake Kua-ta-hu and Caroline—Meditates a terrible revenge.

The bandit chief and his party pursued their way to Sharpe's house. They arrived there the same night that Caroline arrived at Kua-ta-hu's wigwam; but judge of their surprise, and of their deep mortification, when they found Mrs. Sharpe lying upon a bed, unable to articulate a word, or even to comprehend what they said to her. All that they could learn was from the sons of Sharpe. They had gone out to their work, and left the young lady there with their mother. Their mother kept a strict watch upon her, as she said the girl was crazy. They came home at noon, and not finding their mother, they searched the house, and could find no one. They then thought, that as the girl had run away, and been pursued by their mother and brought back, that she might have started again, and that their mother had gone after her. They went out on the same course that their mother had before went, and found her lying, wounded, under a chestnut tree in the edge of the woods. This was all they could learn as to the whereabouts of Caroline. As soon as daylight appeared, they started, and beat about the whole neighborhood. It was evident that the woman had been wounded by a tomahawk, but who had committed the deed? Whoever he was, he had probably carried Caroline away with him, either willingly or unwillingly. They continued to look for Caroline until the next day, when meeting an Indian, they inquired whether he had discovered any one answering to the description of Caroline. He said that a day or two before, he had seen Kua-ta-hu, an Indian that lived alone up the country, going down the river in a canoe, and that there was a "white squaw" with him; and that was all he knew. It was all explained now. Yes, Kua-ta-hu was the man who had rescued her, and it was him that had been seen going down the river in a canoe. All the plans with regard to Miss Mansfield were now frustrated; the bandit chief considered himself now a ruined man; he was no longer safe for a moment; his true character was revealed to Caroline Mansfield. But yet, there might be hope; Kua-ta-hu had never seen him as he knew of, and if Careline had heard nothing from Mrs. Sharpe, he might yet make people believe that he really did rescue her from a band of Indians. He was, however, sorely troubled; he knew not which way to turn, for whatever way he turned innumerable difficulties stared him in the face. He paced up and down with folded arms and lowering brows, and at length, as if the fierce passions that expanded his cheek and darted from his eyes, had burst into a flame, he clutched his tomahawk with desperation, and waving it fiercely about his head, exclaimed, "I have sworn it, and I will perform it! Follow me," said he to his men; and then, with rapid strides, he struck across the country for the cave; he, however, grew calm, and then he talked freely with his men in regard to his plans. The men advised him that probably Kua-ta-hu had carried the girl to his wigwam; they therefore wended their way thither, and arrived there a few hours after Kua-ta-hu had departed. One of the gang, having been much among the Indians, discovered their trail, and with hopes of overtaking them, they pursued it, with the ferocity of blood-hounds; but the track led them finally out upon a road that was lined with occasional houses, and then they were obliged to abandon the pursuit, fearing that they might fall in with some of the parties that might be scouring the country in search of Miss Mansfield. With feelings of bitter disappointment, they turned once more toward the cave, where they arrived soon after. Glanmore finding himself thus foiled, meditated a terrible revenge. All his love for Caroline was now turned into bitter hatred, and as he had all along pleased himself with the idea of finally returning to his own neighborhood—as after he had compelled her into a forced marriage with him, he could probably reconcile her to it—he determined now, in order to avert the impending ruin that would inevitably fall upon him, to make his way to the neighborhood that very night, and before his name should become associated in any way with the transaction of carrying away Caroline, destroy both her and all who should happen to be with her. She would no doubt be at widow ——'s house, with her parents. In the deepest disguise he and his band could assume, they therefore set out, and travelling through the dense forest, came within a few miles of their destination.

CHAPTER XV.

Rushwood arrives safely at the American Camp—Engages in the Battle of Stillwater—Receives the praises of his Fellow-soldiers for his heroic conduct—Is sent out after the Battle to bring in the wounded and dying—Discovers Glanmore's Cousin dead upon the Battle-field, clutching the Letter of Miss Mansfield and his Mother; reads its contents; is filled with gloomy forebodings—Engages in another Battle—Follows Arnold in his headlong and courageous Charge upon the Enemy.

When Lieut. Rushwood arrived at the American camp, all was bustle and confusion; they were preparing to go forth to the battle-field to meet in deadly conflict Burgoyne's trusty legions. George hastened to join his division, and then, with a brave heart that never flinched or cowed before danger, he rode forth to the battle-field, thinking only of victory and Caroline Mansfield; and there, amid the terrible carnage of that terrific encounter, he rode down the foeman, and passed unscathed until the conflict ended. He received the highest encomiums from his brother officers; and when around the camp-fires the war-worn veterans and raw militia reverted to the deeds of daring that had been that day performed, none received a greater share of praise, justly merited, than Lieut. Rushwood.

Next day he was sent with a detachment to bury the bodies of some of the principal officers that had fallen, as well as to bring in those of the wounded Americans that might not have been discovered. While passing among the slain that were lying in ghastly death, thickly strewn upon the ground, he was struck with the appearance of a soldier that lay dead upon the ground firmly clutching a letter in his closely-clenched hands. George glanced at the letter, and to his infinite surprise and astonishment saw that it was addressed to him, and in Caroline Mansfield's handwriting. He took it from the dead man's grasp, and there, for the first time, read these encouraging lines, that Caroline had penned, and also the part from his mother. He examined the countenance of the man closely; it was not the soldier that had carried his letter. There was some mystery here. He examined the countenance again; he had it now—yes; this man was a cousin to Glanmore. There was something in the transaction that boded fearfully, and although elated with victory, yet a heavy load rested upon his heart.

Time, with ever-revolving wheels, sped on and stopt. George would fain have gone home, yet he could get no opportunity. At length, the 7th of October, 1777, was ushered in, and with it the thunder of the British cannon. George again went forth to the battle-field, and there again he mingled with the hosts of Burgoyne in deadly conflict. There was the gallant Fraser urging on his forces, and there was also the brave, the impetuous, the terrible Arnold, clearing like a thunderbolt through the battle-field. Now encouraging the Americans in one place, now in another, and again rushing with furious and headlong recklessness—they, the finest of both armies: and when, near sundown, that terribly excited warrior gathered about him some of his best troops, and rushed furiously against the British, none rode more fearlessly or daringly at his heels than the brave and intrepid Lieut. Rushwood. But night put an end to that terrible struggle, and our hero escaped again unhurt, save a slight sabre wound, that gave him a scar forever afterwards, on his right hand.

Fresh from these victorious battle-fields, he set out in a few days for his home. He was uncertain whether he should find any one there, as the inhabitants, terror-stricken, had fled from their habitations towards Albany; but they were now returning, and with light hearts they greeted him as he rode along home with a few of his brave fellows, that he had brought with him to assist in expelling the straggling Tories from the country. As he came within a few miles of his home, he made some inquiries respecting his mother and her neighbors; but the only intelligence he could get was, that Mr. Mansfield's house had been robbed and he killed, and his daughter carried off by the Indians. The news fell like a thunderbolt upon him. Plunging his spurs into his horse's sides, he rode onwards towards the scene of destruction, with about the same degree of recklessness that Arnold had exhibited at Bemis Heights, and arrived at the scene of destruction with his followers just after dark. He halted not—no, he wished not now to gaze upon the ashes of the house from whence his betrothed had been rudely borne captive.

His mother, hearing the thundering of the troops as they came furiously onward towards her house, was terrified at first; but when they halted at the door, she again heard that soul-cheering neigh. But her son came not as he came before—all mildness, all tenderness. No; he was wild now, frantic with rage, and thirsting for vengeance upon his foes, who had wrested the object of his heart from her parents' arms, and left them in the embrace of death. He rushed into the house, followed by his mother. With hurried and impatient steps he paced the floor, requesting her to tell him all she knew about the fate of Caroline Mansfield.

The old lady, who was, to tell the truth, a little jealous that George had taken little or no notice of her, and seemed to centre his whole mind upon Miss Mansfield, exclaimed, in a half serious, half joking way, "Why, George, these young men who have come with you will really think that you was engaged to be married to Caroline, you make such a prodigious fuss about her."

"Mother," said he, emphatically, "I was betrothed to her;" and, drawing his heavy sword, he swung it in a fearful circle over his head, and again exclaimed, with a thundering tone, "Yes, I was betrothed; she was all the world to me; and woe to the man or men that have carried her away and murdered her brave old father; woe to them, if they ever come within the reach of this trusty sword!"

"Hush, George!" said the old lady; "Mr. Mansfield is in the next room: he is not dead, but very ill."

"Thank God!" exclaimed George; and in an instant he was at the bedside of Mr. Mansfield.

Both were too full for a moment to speak. As to old Mrs. Mansfield, she had heard the rout when the young troopers came, and when she looked out of the door and saw them stalk in with their shining swords and war-worn and sunburnt countenances, her imagination converted them into Indians. She was so much affrighted, that she did not comprehend what had been said by George; but as soon as she recognized him, it seemed as though she could no longer contain herself. She threw her arms around his neck and wept like an infant; for she well knew the deep affection that he entertained for her daughter. And now she felt as though she had wronged the noble youth in objecting to his suit, and would fain endeavor to make amends for so doing.

After the first blush of excitement was over, Mr. Mansfield related to George the whole transaction at his house on the fatal night when his beloved and only child was torn from him. When he recovered from the stunning effects of the blow he had received from the tomahawk, he found himself lying in his bed-room, and it was already filled with smoke; he felt his wife lying near him. Comprehending his danger, he made a desperate effort to escape. He heard the flame crackling in the ceiling of the next room that the door of the bed-room led into: he knew from the smoke already in the bed-room, that if he opened the door, he would be suffocated. There was no window to the bed-room; it being merely a small slit just large enough to set a bed in—(a thing common in old-fashioned country houses)—it was separated from the other room by only a single upright board partition. He threw himself against that with all his force, and, being a heavy man, it gave way before him, and in a few moments he made an opening through it. He drew his insensible wife after him, and escaped through a window of that room into the open air. Leaving his wife at some distance, he returned to search for his daughter; but she could not be found. The interior of the house was all on fire, and he could not enter. Crazed with his wound and great excitement, he knew nothing more until he found himself lying on a bed in Mrs. Rushwood's house, where he now was. Search had been made for his daughter, but it was of no avail. Kua-ta-hu had been there, but he knew nothing of any band of Indians.

"There is some mystery in all this," said George. "I believe these men were a band of Tories headed by Gordon Glanmore."

He then related the circumstance of his being attacked while going back to the army, and also the circumstances attending the discovery of the letter, and wound up by saying that he believed that Caroline could be found yet—at all events, when morning dawned he should make an effort.

"I overheard what you said to your mother, George," said Mansfield; "I freely forgive you and Caroline for your rashness in betrothing yourselves without my knowledge. And now, my noble boy," said he, taking George's hand, "she is yours by my consent, since you have proved yourself by your gallant conduct on the field of battle worthy of her, as soon as we can recover her. If we never find her, you shall be my adopted son at all events."

While they were thus speaking, a rap was heard at the door. George went to it, and opening it, whom should he see standing there but Kua-ta-hu, and behind him a slightly-formed young Indian. Kua-ta-hu seemed overjoyed to meet George, and gave him a squeeze of the hand that was really of a warm and feeling nature. Kua-ta-hu entered the house, and the young Indian followed and timidly seated himself in one corner where the light fell but sparingly on his face. Kua-ta-hu remained silent. At length, the young Indian got up, and with a graceful fawn-like step, was about to enter the bed-room where Mr. Mansfield lay. In an instant the troopers, who had eyed these Indians with distrust, sprung forward to prevent his entry. George caught hold of him; and in the excitement of the moment, the balance of the troop did not hear the thrilling accent of that voice, as it whispered to their Lieutenant, "George, it is I!" They started back with amazement as they saw him throw his arms around the young savage, and imprint a kiss upon his brow. George waved them back with his hand, and supporting the now trembling form of Caroline to her father's bedside, he restored to his arms his lost daughter.

Disguised and disfigured as she was, they recognized her features; and now their cup of happiness was full. They were indeed a happy family, united as they were now under one roof. Mr. Mansfield and his wife were rejoiced to find their lost daughter; old Mrs. Rushwood was rejoiced to behold her gallant son at home once more safe and sound; and above all, George and Caroline were unspeakably happy to have the privilege of meeting under such favorable auspices.

Caroline retired to another room and changed her Indian costume for a more Christian attire, and having exchanged her bedaubed countenance for the rose that now bloomed upon her lovely cheek, she was led blushing back into the room, by Rushwood, where the young troopers were, and introduced to them as Miss Caroline Mansfield. The truth now flashed upon their minds—she was the young Indian. Oh! they now understood why Lieut. Rushwood kissed him so tenderly; and then the rude, the brave, the boisterous and victorious young American soldiers sent up three such loud and prolonged cheers for Lieut. Rushwood and his beautiful betrothed as never were heard before under Widow Rushwood's roof.

"I rather think," said one of them, "that Miss Mansfield will suppose that Lieut. Rushwood has not learned us much good manners, after such boisterous behavior as this."

"O! sir," said Caroline, "I am so overwhelmed with all this good fortune, that I feel very much like crying, myself; and now that you have bravely defeated Burgoyne, you may rest assured that we American ladies will be disposed to overlook all your outbursts of joy, however out of place they may be. You will, hereafter, be entitled to great privileges."

Having become quieted all around, and the first wild tumult of surprise, of joy and happiness being passed, the whole company sat down, and Caroline related all she had heard and seen, from the time of her capture, to the time of her arrival at Widow Rushwood's. Kua-ta-hu then gave an account of the discovery of the cave, and of all his subsequent discoveries. When they had made an end of speaking, George Rushwood exclaimed, "It is all out now. Glanmore never went to New York; he has never been a prisoner there; and it is he that has headed the gang of Tories, disguised as Indians, that have robbed and murdered so many this summer. And above all, it was he that robbed and burned Mr. Mansfield's house. Base, black-hearted traitor, robber and murderer!—he is unfit to live—he must be taken prisoner before to-morrow's sunset, yes, before to-morrow's sun shall set, this gang will be our prisoners, and their dark hiding-place will be destroyed!"

"My friends," said Mr. Mansfield to the young men, "I wish you to bear me witness, that I humbly ask pardon of Lieut. Rushwood, for preferring a man who has turned out such a villainous traitor, before him, as a suitor of my daughter; and as she and George have wisely taken the matter into their own hands, I now make him all the amends in my power, by freely giving my consent to their union. Come here, my children," said he to George and Caroline, and joining their hands as he lay on the bed, he blessed them. The youth who had in a few short months been converted into the hardy warrior, that could send his sword with dreadful power to the heart of an enemy, was melted, the tears rolled down his cheeks, while the fair and lovely Caroline fell upon her knees and thanked her Heavenly Father that every impediment to their union was now removed.

CHAPTER XVII.

Widow Rushwood's house attacked by a band of men—They are defeated by Rushwood and his party—Terrible race after their leader—His fate—George and Caroline united in matrimony—End of Kua-ta-hu.

THE plans for the expedition of the next day were now laid out; the company retired for the night, with the exception of one, who was left as a sentinel; Lieut. Rushwood deeming it necessary to keep a strict watch, as it was probable that he might be attacked during that night by some unseen and lurking foe; and as he had now attained "the pearl of great price," that he had been so long laboring for, he was determined to take every precaution in order to keep her safely, until his enemies should be secured. At length, all were sunk into that sweet and sound sleep that occurs after long and continued anxiety.

The young man who had been posted as sentinel, looking anxiously about, imagined that he saw a single person stealing towards the house, and just behind him another. He placed himself in a position where he could see the movements of these strange persons. They cautiously approached the house, and skulking around the corners, listened as if endeavoring to hear if any one was stirring within; at length they came very near where the sentinel lay concealed: he heard them say in a whisper:—

"To-night will be the time, there does not appear to be any one here, the old widow, and old Mansfield and his wife, are most likely all the persons in the house. If Kua-ta-hu has got home with the girl, we will have all safe, though if we get him penned up, he will be an ugly customer."

"Suppose," said the other, "that George should be here, would it not be well for us to go to the barn and see whether there is any horses there? They never kept but one horse, and that George took into the army. If we find a horse there I can tell whether it is his."

"You are too cautious," said the other, "cannot seven overpower two? Never mind the horses; let's go back and arouse the men, and if the fates do not disappoint us, in one hour from this time we will put an end to this matter."

They then turned away, and went rapidly towards a neighboring road. The sentinel trembled lest they should go to the barn and discover the horses that filled the stable, and the military trappings that lay thickly strewn upon the barn floor, as they might perhaps take the alarm, and render it difficult to capture them. But now that they were coming to attack the house, he hastened, as soon as they were gone, to arouse Lieut. Rushwood and the six young men, who were asleep. They proceeded with the utmost caution to make arrangements to receive the prowling Tories, as they doubted not, from the conversation overheard by the sentinel, they were. The women and Mr. Mansfield were all removed to the cellar, as then they would be out of the way of balls, if any should be fired into the house. Two men were sent to saddle all the horses, so as to have them ready to pursue them if they attempted to escape. Having completed all their arrangements in a short space of time, they posted themselves at a little distance from the house, behind such things as they could, to avoid being seen. Kua-ta-hu was posted away at a little distance farther, to give the alarm when he should hear them coming. He lay with his ear close to the ground, and it was not many minutes before he came close by the men, and gave the signal of alarm. Closely now each brave fellow nestled in his hiding-place, and firmly grasped his weapons. They had counted on close fighting, and were armed only with swords and pistols; except Kua-ta-hu, who was armed with a long rifle, and a tomahawk. The women crouched in the cellar, momentarily expecting to hear the death-shot, that might send some one of the gallant party, who had determined to defend them, into eternity.

At length, the men began to hear the softly-approaching footsteps of the assailants. Nearer and nearer came they—passing so near Lieut. Rushwood, that he could have struck the nearest down without moving from where he stood.

"Now, remember," said one, in a very low tone, "the orders are, to save the girl and bring her to the chief, who is posted down the road with a horse to carry her off."

"I should have thought," returned another, "that he had got

enough of that. He is a consummate fool: for my part, if the girl comes in my reach, I'll make an end of her."

"Remember your oaths, men," said the one who appeared to be leader, "and obey the chief. You know he loves the girl, and cannot make up his mind to kill her."

They moved on a few feet, and were about to separate for the purpose of surrounding the house, when, quick as lightning, they were surrounded by the brave troopers; and the glaring broadswords done the work so successfully, that in two minutes not one of them was left standing. Not a shot was fired, and so silently did the work of death proceed, that nothing above a groan and the clash of the swords was heard. The bandaleros were struck dumb at seeing themselves so suddenly surrounded by men in military costume; and, paralyzed with guilt and fear, offered but little or no resistance.

Instantly, as soon as the young men had done, Lieut. Rushwood said to his men: "We have more work to do; did you not hear them say that the chief was posted down the road with a horse to carry the girl away? Here, Kua-ta-hu," said he, "you go in the direction that the party came from, and see if you can discover him; if you do, come back and let us know immediately. But hist! I hear the tramp of a horse. I think he has got impatient, and is coming to see what his men are about. Quick—here! four of you to horse with me, and let's pursue him, while the others stay here and look to the bodies and guard the house. Kua-ta-hu, keep an eye on him, and see if you can make him out;" and so saying, the Lieutenant, with four of his followers, stepped quickly and lightly to the barn, where they vaulted into their saddles.

They were not much more than mounted before Kua-ta-hu came back, and assured them that he recognized the man on horseback as Glanmore; that he seemed to be approaching towards the house, and was evidently uneasy about the issue of the attack upon it. Kua-ta-hu assured George that he could easily shoot him with his rifle, if he wished it. But George refused, saying, "That he wished, by all means to take him alive; and at the same time ordered his men not to shoot him when they came up with him, unless it became, for the preservation of their own lives, absolutely necessary."

They then rode in single file slowly down the road, and in a few moments discovered a man on horseback standing by the side of the road. He had undoubtedly heard them, and supposed them to be his men; but no sooner did he discover what they were, than he sped away down the road like lightning.

The troopers plunged their spurs deeply into the horses, and then commenced a fearful chase. The horse rode by the bandit was a strong active sorrel that had attained his seventh year without being broken, only to the saddle: he carried his rider forward like the wind. The horses of the troopers ran not so fast on the start, but having been fed principally on grain, were longer winded and better trotters; and after a few miles began to gain on the horse of the bandit. Several times he made up his mind to abandon his horse and trust to his legs across the country; but the eager troopers pressed him so closely, that it seemed impracticable for him to escape in that way.

Long did that fearful chase continue. The horse of the fugitive was covered with foam, and the sweat fell from him in large drops. The troopers' horses were also flecked with foam, and the blood trickled down their sides from the wounds made by the sharp spurs.

At length, the morn peered up from the eastern horizon, and then the terrified bandit looked over his shoulder and saw the five horsemen plainly, and heard their shout, and knew the voice of his rival. Death now stared him in the face; he would gladly have turned and measured swords with his rival, but he was alone—and why should he throw away his life against such fearful odds? No! he must fly; his horse was giving out. He faltered—he fell! Springing from his back, he plunged into a dark pine wood. He heard the roaring of the Mohawk. Was it possible he had come so far?

He was not aware of his being so near the river, although he had ridden far and rapidly.

No sooner had the troopers reached the spot where his horse lay, than they dismounted, and, without standing to fasten their horses, dropped the bridles, and taking each a pistol from his holster, plunged into the woods after Glanmore.

He ran violently away, but did not succeed in getting out of their sight. He reached the high ridge above the Mohawk, and his pursuers gained fearfully upon him. He halted a moment, resolved to sell his life as dearly as possible. But when he saw the five determined men coming with desperate haste towards him, he determined to make another effort to save his life and secure his liberty.

The Mohawk was high and rapid now since the heavy rains. He had an advantage over his pursuers—he could throw off his blanket, and be comparatively free to swim; while his pursuers, encumbered by their uniforms, would not probably attempt to pursue him: he might probably reach the opposite shore, by swimming with the stream: he was sure his pursuers had no fire-arms, except pistols, and he could get out of the reach of their fire before they reached the bank.

These thoughts crowded through his mind with the rapidity of lightning; and, urged on by a last hope of escape, he ran furiously towards the river and rushed into the water. But alas, for him! he had mistaken the force of the current; for no sooner did he reach the main current, than it swept him fearfully down, and, diverging into two branches, one of them carried him in a diagonal direction, and, although he struggled against it, brought him so near the shore, that his pursuers, who were on the bluffs above, following along and watching his progress, could have shot him with their pistols.

"Lieutenant, he struggles manfully," said one of the men to George; "don't you think we might better shoot him now, that he is within reach, for you see he may get across the river?"

"No, I will not shoot him. It is impossible for him to cross the river. See! he appears to be sinking now—no; there! he has seized upon an old tree that is floating down the stream. I would like to take him prisoner. But see! how swiftly he goes down stream!—Follow, men."

And then they kept pace with him along the high rocks that overlook the north side of the Mohawk above the Cohoes Falls.

Yes, he had already begun to near the rapid current above the falls. The thunder of the vast volume of water, that here tumbled seventy feet down the high rocks thrown across the Mohawk, struck like a death-knell upon his ears; and although Lieut. Rushwood would have sent his sword crashing through his brain, while in the eager excitement of the chase, yet as he stood now upon the shore, and calmly assured of the near approach of the most bitter and unrelenting enemy that ever crossed his path, to a death awful to contemplate, he would fain have plunged into the dark-rolling waters and rescued him; but it would have been of no avail, for the fearful current bore him rapidly, and more rapidly, down; until at length the log, to which he clung with the desperation of a drowning man, shot with the swiftness of an arrow down the stream, and coming to the edge of the falls, plunged down into the foaming abyss below. The terrified and appalled bandit uttered a wild shriek, but it was drowned by the tremendous roaring of the angry waters; and thus died one who might have been an honor to his country, but who had been led on by the fierce and bitter passions of his nature, fostered and trained by a parent, who ought to have suffered in his stead.

After the bandit had gone down the foaming falls, the troopers took their stand some distance below, expecting to see his mangled body borne down the stream by the angry current. They tarried until after daylight, but discovering nothing, they hurried back towards the place where they had left their horses: when they came to the spot, the horses were gone. They saw that their tracks led back the way they had come. The troopers were afraid of losing their horses, but Lieut. Rushwood assured them that his horse would lead them safely back to his house. They had not gone far, before they were met by a party of the neighbors, who had been aroused, and had come in pursuit of them. They arrived at the house about sundown, to the great relief of their friends, who, having seen the horses come back without riders, were greatly alarmed lest the whole party had been killed.

Being now all assembled around a cheerful fire, the particulars of the chase were given, and the fearful death of the bandit closed the narrative. All the men that had been cut down the night before, by the sabres of the troopers, were dead and buried; except Sharpe, who had been cared for, and was likely to recover. Next morning he was found to be able to speak. He was promised, that if he would give a history of the whole of the transactions of the band, and would agree to leave that part of the country as soon as he recovered, his life would be spared. He sullenly refused to give any account of the gang, and feigning to be deranged, and very sick with his wounds, succeeded in making his escape three days afterwards.

Early next morning, a large party, consisting of Lieut. Rushwood, as leader, the young troopers, and some neighbors, who had joined them, guided by Kua-ta-hu, set out for the cave, at Snake Hill, and there within its gloomy recess, found hidden all the ill-gotten, and blood-bought gold of the bandits. Mr. Mansfield's money was found just as the robbers had taken it, it having been kept out of the common stock for the chief. The cave was destroyed, and now no traces of it can be seen, as the rubbish and dirt washed down the hill by the storm-torrents soon filled up its cavity. The lofty pine, that had served as a ventilator to the cave, weakened by the incisions made in its top, fell the next year, before a terrific tornado that swept across the lake.

The party returned to the Widow Rushwood's house, and there the money taken from the cave was counted, and found to amount to a large sum. It was left in the care of George, who, after considerable trouble, succeeded in restoring most of it to the families of those from whom it had been taken.

The gallant Lieut. Rushwood, victorious at all points, led the beautiful Caroline Mansfield to the hymeneal altar a few days afterwards. The two families that had by the fates been thus united under one roof, continued to live there until the thundering of the British artillery had been silenced at Yorktown, and the American flag waved triumphant over their war-worn, but now happy and grateful country. A substantial mansion was then erected on the ruins of Mr. Mansfield's farm-house, and the two happy families live there in peace and plenty—George employing his time in cultivating the broad acres of the domain that had now become his; and Caroline in training up a family of blooming children in the "way they should go." The old people lived to see their grand-children smile upon the savages, before they sunk in their peaceful graves.

But the old Tory, terrified at the capture of his son, fled with his wife to the British army, and finally embarked for England, where he died a victim to that deep remorse, that ever haunts those who thus step aside from the path of virtuous rectitude.

The faithful and noble Kua-ta-hu, was solicited by his grateful friends, to abandon his wild mode of life, and take up his residence under their hospitable roof; but he was too deeply wedded to his native wild woods, to think of abandoning them; and above all, he had acquired so strong an appetite for the waters of the High Rock Spring, that after living away from them a few days, he seemed to be out of his element. After a few years the place began to be settled, and old age having dimmed his sight, and enervated his arm, he made his way to Lieut. Rushwood's mansion, where in a few months he yielded up his life, and was buried by his grateful friends in the family burying-ground, where rested the body of Mr. Mansfield.

THE END.

FORTUNE-TELLERS, DREAM-BOOKS, Etc.

Complete Fortune-Teller and Dream-Book; or, an Infallible Guide to the Hidden Decrees of Fate. By MADAME CONNOISSEUR, First of the Seven Wise Mistresses of Rome. Being a new and regular system for foretelling Future Events by Dreams, Moles, etc., etc. Also, The Oraculum; or, Napoleon's Book of Fate, from an ancient Egyptian Manuscript, found in the Royal Tombs, in Upper Egypt. **Price 35 cents.**

A New and Complete Dream-Book, Fortune-Teller, Dial of Fate, and Oraculum; the whole forming an unerring guide to the knowledge of Future Events. *Contents:* Dreams, Moles, The Moon, Physiognomy, Cards, Grounds of Coffee, Charms and Ceremonies, Spells and Incantations, etc. **Price 35 cents.**

Sibylline Oracles; or, Dreams and their Interpretations; being the **Spanish Fate Book,** containing, also, Napoleon's Oraculum and Fortune-Teller; being the rules by which he is said to have guided his actions during his unparalleled career, until, at last, disregarding its warnings, he fell. 32mo, **Price 35 cents.**

The Sibyl's Cave; or, Book of Oracles, (Fortune-Telling by questions answered from the Poets,) for ladies and gentlemen. Selected and arranged by MRS. ANNE BACKE. 32mo, cloth. **Price 25 cents.**

RATTLEHEAD'S HUMOROUS WORKS.

Life and Adventures of an Arkansaw Doctor, by DAVID RATTLEHEAD, M. D., (the Man of Scrapes.) Handsomely illustrated; illuminated cover. **Price 50 cents.**

This is one of the most humorous and laughter-provoking books of the age. The recital of the Doctor's numerous scrapes—the easy, familiar style of telling, all conspire to make it a pleasant companion for traveling or home reading.

Rattlehead's Travels; or, the Recollections of a Backwoodsman, who has traveled many Thousand Miles on the Highways of Human Destiny; brought about a Revolution in Domestic Happiness, and effected a general Shake-up of Creation. By DAVID RATTLEHEAD, M. D., (the Man of Scrapes,) author of the "Arkansaw Doctor," etc., etc. Illustrated; fancy cover. **Price 50 cents.**

Redstick; or, Scenes in the South, by B. R. MONTESANO, Esq., of Louisiana. Octavo, illustrated cover. **Price 25 cents.**

A highly amusing and humorous book—full of fun and practical jokes.

"If any of our readers wish to enjoy a good, hearty, genuine laugh, they have only to buy the book and read it."—*Chronicle.*

EMERSON BENNETT'S POPULAR NOVELS.

The Prairie Flower; or, Adventures in the Far West. By EMERSON BENNETT. New edition, revised and corrected by the author. 8vo, paper cover. **Price 25 cents.**

Leni Leoti; a Sequel to "Prairie Flower;" new edition. 8vo, paper cover. **Price 25 cents.**

Works of the most exciting interest from beginning to end—full of incident and stirring life. The celebrated Kit Carson figures conspicuously.

The Forest Rose, a tale of the Frontier, by EMERSON BENNETT. 8vo, paper cover. **Price 25 cents.**

Mike Fink, a legend of the Ohio, by EMERSON BENNETT. 8vo, paper cover. **Price 25 cents.**

Ella Barnwell, a Historical Romance of Border Life, by EMERSON BENNETT. 8vo, paper cover. **Price 25 cents.**

The three last are thrilling stories of border life. The leading characters and events are from actual history—Daniel Boone, Simon Kenton, Lewis Wetzel, Mike Fink, and the renegade Simon Girty, are prominent characters in the different books.

The Female Spy; or, Treason in the Camp: a story of the Revolution. 8vo, paper cover **Price 25 cents.**

Rosalie du Pont, a Sequel to "Female Spy." 8vo, paper cover. **Price 25 cents.**

The Fair Rebel, a tale of Colonial Times. 8vo, paper cover. **Price 25 cents.**

The Traitor; or, The Fate of Ambition. 8vo, paper cover; **Price 75 cents.**

The Bandits of the Osage, a Western Romance. 8vo, paper cover. **Price 25 cents.**

The League of the Miami. 8vo, paper cover. **Price 25 cents.**

The Mysterious Marksman; or, The Outlaws of New York. 8vo, paper cover. **Price 25 cents.**

The Unknown Countess; or, Crime and its Results. 8vo, paper cover. **Price 25 cents.**

Few writers of romance and fiction have the good fortune to suit the taste of the reading public as completely as Emerson Bennett. His name has become a household word, and his writings are eagerly sought for everywhere. There is in them something stirring, yet natural and lifelike—his descriptions, whether of persons or scenery, are vivid, and the reader has before him, in his mind's eye, all the varied events almost as clearly as though they were enacting in his very presence; while nothing can be found in them to offend the most fastidious.

MISS ELIZA A. DUPUY'S NOVELS.

Emma Walton; or, Trials and Triumph. 8vo, paper cover. **Price 50 cents.**

Annie Seldon; or, The Concealed Treasure. 8vo, paper cover. **Price 25 cents.**

Miss Dupuy's name is familiar to the readers of fiction throughout the Union, and deservedly so; for in addition to a fluent and natural style, by which she is at once at home with her readers, a happy faculty of delineation and description, and just conception of the probable and the possible, eschewing humdrum improbabilities, ever avoiding vulgarity of sentiment or expression, her writings tend to the inculcation of virtue and morality.

SIR E. L. BULWER'S BEST NOVELS.

The Last Days of Pompeii. 8vo, paper cover. **Price 50 cents.**

Eugene Aram. 8vo, paper cover. **Price 50 cents.**

Pelham; or, the Adventures of a Gentleman. 8vo, paper cover. **Price 50 cents.**

Ernest Maltravers. 8vo, paper cover. **Price 50 cents.**

Alice; or, The Mysteries: a Sequel to Ernest Maltravers. 8vo, paper cover. **Price 50 cents.**

The Lady of Lyons; or, Love and Pride: a Play in Five Acts. Paper cover. **Price 15 cents.**

Zanoni, a Romance of Italy. 8vo, paper cover. **Price 50 cents.**

Godolphin. 8vo, paper cover. **Price 50 cents.**

ALEX. DUMAS'S NOVELS.

The Convert of Saint Paul, a tale of Greece and Rome; translated by Henry W. Herbert, Esq. 8vo, paper cover. **Price 25 cents.**

Louisa; or, Adventures of a French Milliner; translated by J. Griswold. 8vo, paper cover. **Price 50 cents.**

HENRY COCKTON'S NOVELS.

[AUTHOR OF VALENTINE VOX, ETC.]

The Love Match, designed to illustrate the various conflicting influences which sprang from the union of Mr. and Mrs. Tom Todd. 8vo, paper cover. **Price 50 cents.**

The Prince; or, George St. George Julian. 8vo, paper cover. **Price 75 cents.**

EDWIN F. ROBERT'S NOVELS.

The Twin Brothers; or, The Victims of the Press-Gang, a Romance of the Land and Sea. 8vo, paper cover. **Price 25 cents.**

The Road to Ruin; or, The Dangers of the Town, a Career of Crime. 8vo, paper cover. **Price 25 cents.**

G. P. R. JAMES'S BEST NOVELS.

One in a Thousand; or, The Days of Henry IV. 8vo, paper cover. **Price 50 cents.**

Richelieu, a tale of France. 8vo, paper cover. **Price 50 cents.**

The Robber. 8vo, paper cover. **Price 50 cents.**

Philip Augustus; or, The Brothers in Arms. 8vo, paper cover. **Price 50 cents.**

The Gipsy. 8vo, paper cover. **Price 50 cents.**

The Ancient Regime; or, Annette de St. Morin. 8vo, paper cover. **Price 50 cents.**

The Gentleman of the Old School. 8vo, paper cover. **Price 50 cents.**

"Richelieu is one of the most spirited, amusing, and interesting romances I ever read."—*Prof. Wilson.*

"His romances are almost entirely founded on historical facts, and the subjects drawn from every age and clime."

EUGENE SUE'S BEST NOVELS.

Latreaumont; or, The Conspiracy: a Historical Romance of the days of Louis XIV; translated from the French. 8vo, paper cover. **Price 50 cents.**

The Temptation; or, The Duchess of Almeda: a Romantic Tale; translated from the French. 8vo, paper cover. **Price 25 cents.**

The Princess of Hansfeld, a Story of Love and Intrigue; translated from the French. 8vo, paper cover. **Price 25 cents.**

The Commander of Malta, with illustrations. 8vo, paper cover. **Price 25 cents.**

GOOD BOOKS, BY VARIOUS AUTHORS.

A Man Made of Money, by Douglas Jerrold, editor of "Punch," "Mrs. Caudle's Lectures," etc. 8vo, paper cover. **Price 25 cents.**

www.ingramcontent.com/pod-product-compliance
Lightning Source LLC
LaVergne TN
LVHW021428110826
845150LV00007B/2141

* 9 7 8 1 4 2 5 5 0 7 1 4 5 *